MASTER YOUR DESTINY
Lessons From Lohani

MASTER YOUR DESTINY
Lessons From Lohani

Chronicle of a Civil Servant's Journey

Tarun Pithode

PRABHAT
PRAKASHAN

Published by
PRABHAT PRAKASHAN PVT. LTD.
4/19 Asaf Ali Road,
New Delhi-110 002 (INDIA)
e-mail: prabhatbooks@gmail.com

ISBN 978-93-5562-830-5
MASTER YOUR DESTINY: Lessons From Lohani
by Shri Tarun Pithode

Edition
First, 2024

Paperback Price
₹ 300.00 (Rupees Three Hundred only)

Printed at
R-Tech Offset Printers, Delhi

Acknowledgement

I started my career in Indian Administrative Services hearing a lot about Ashwani Lohani and my book on Covid offered me an opportunity to interact with him. I started learning from his experiences as I interacted with him more and more. I must thank him for the time he gave me to take his interviews which form the basis of this book and for the permission to publish the book.

I would like to thank M.P. Bezbaruah, V.K. Duggal, Arun Dhar, Sanjay Gupta, Ajit Bajaj, Naveen Berry, Aditya Ghosh, Harbhajan Singh, Subhash Goyal, Naresh Kapuria, Meenakshi Mallik, Rajaji, Ramesh Katiyar, Ajay Singh, Shalini Diwan, Jyoti Mayal, H.R. Jagannath, Vinay Sanan, Ajit Bhaskar and Pawan Sharma who despite their tight schedule, took time to speak to me and happily agreed to share their experiences of working with Ashwani Lohani for the book.

I am also thankful to Yamini V. Ashar and Akrati Pithode for the sketches and the whole editorial team whose invaluable feedback helped make this book happen.

I am thankful to my family for their continued support while I was working on this book.

Introduction

Ever wondered what sets certain individuals apart, propelling them to heights most can only dream of? What's the secret sauce for success—career, friendships, wealth, or the goodwill we leave behind? Why do some people stay etched in our memories while others fade away? These questions have long been on my mind.

Last year, I had the chance to meet someone I'd heard much about and always wanted to meet: Ashwani Lohani, a legend in public management and administration, a record-holder and a successful civil servant known for his stellar performance. After our first meeting, it became clear that there was much to learn from him, not just for me, but for anyone aiming to excel in management.

When you're passionate about achieving something and the path isn't crystal clear, following in the footsteps of those who've walked it before is wise. A person inclined to learn realises that what he knows isn't enough, yet sometimes, one person's life is sufficient to teach how to excel. The lessons I gained from Ashwani Lohani are, in my view, worth sharing with everyone.

Hence, this compelled me to pen down and share his stories, hoping they enrich others' understanding as they did mine.

Leadership isn't always an innate trait; many become leaders through experience and upbringing. This led me to explore the style of parenting and experiences that mould a person into a successful leader. But, before delving into Ashwani Lohani's tales of struggle and triumph, let's take a peek into his school days to uncover the ingredients that earned him respect from peers, seniors, juniors, friends and family.

Ashwani Lohani hails from an educated family of Kanpur, with his father, Dr. Basant Kumar Lohani, an esteemed textile expert, and his mother, Krishna Lohani, a postgraduate in English. Sadly, his sister, Kumkum ,Lohani, who was a year older, is no longer with us. Growing up, his parents read him a story every night, providing guidance on his career. His entire family played a crucial role in shaping his successful career, even though they are no longer with him.

Recalling his father's advice before heading to Jamalpur, a renowned textile engineer of his time, Lohani shared, "Son, learn to differentiate between what is yours and what is not." This piece of wisdom stuck with him.

Lohani's love affair with steam locomotives began in infancy, thanks to his father taking him to Kanpur railway station. There, he marvelled at steam locomotives, guided by a loco pilot-friend who gave him a peek into the engine's interiors, allowing him to try pulling the whistle cord—an early introduction to the fascinating world of railways.

Lohani, a boy of simplicity, soft demeanour and disciplined habits, attended St. Aloysius School for his Senior Cambridge education and completed his schooling in 1973. Continuing his academic journey, he completed his Intermediate from Christ Church Inter College in Kanpur. Contrary to being a class topper, Lohani recalls his school days with fondness, acknowledging that he was a diligent student but not the foremost achiever. However, his experience at Jamalpur, where he observed his batch-mates excelling, fuelled a determination to prove his mettle and strive for excellence.

In his early school days, Lohani grappled with a timid personality, harbouring fears of the dark, ghosts and school bullies. To confront his anxieties, around the age of 12, he embarked on a daring quest. Without informing his parents, he spent an hour sitting on a grave at the Muslim cemetery in Gwaltoli at 7 in the evening, resulting in the vanquishing of his fears.

During his childhood, Subodh was Lohani's closest friend and their bond extended from playful childhood days to shared study sessions. From Subodh, Lohani imbibed the lesson that courage transcends physical strength, emphasising that it emanates from the mind. Subodh's early departure from life left a void that Lohani still feels every day.

Despite not being a class-topper, Lohani secured a first division in both the Senior Cambridge and Intermediate examinations of the UP Board. Influenced by his father, he initially pursued Textile Engineering after the Intermediate examination but eventually found his calling in the Special Class Railway Apprentices (SCRA)

Examination in 1975. Joining Jamalpur in February 1976, this examination was considered prestigious, as many top Railway Board officials hailed from the SCRA background.

Vinay Sanan, Lohani's schoolmate and close companion, attested to Lohani's exceptional observance and intelligence from their early years. Describing him as unassuming and cool, Sanan highlighted Lohani's knack for providing solutions to challenging questions. While other classmates engaged in typical teenage antics, Lohani maintained a studious, quiet demeanour, earning the respect of his peers.

Continuing his academic journey, Lohani pursued engineering at the Indian Railways Institute of Mechanical and Electrical Engineering, Jamalpur. As part of his training with IRSME, he delved into mechanical, electrical, metallurgical, electronics and telecommunication engineering.

"In my childhood, I always dreamt of setting records—ecords that would get me recognition and an elevated status in the eyes of others," shares Ashwani Lohani. He cherished attention and dreamt of achieving something monumental. Upon completing Senior Cambridge and Intermediate, Lohani arrived at Jamalpur as a special class apprentice of the railways, despite lacking the academic accolades that many of his peers possessed.

While many of his batch-mates at Jamalpur were Board-level toppers and rankers, Lohani found himself with fewer accomplishments, a realisation that lingered in his mind. The examination requirements at Jamalpur demanded clearing mechanical engineering exams held by the Institution of Mechanical Engineers, London, or the Institution of Engineers, India. Students typically cleared additional examinations, especially in electrical engineering.

In a remarkable feat, Lohani cleared four engineering degrees—mechanical, electrical, metallurgical and electronics & telecommunication engineering— almost three months before his graduation in February 1980. Proudly, under twenty-one years of age, he stood as perhaps the only individual in the world armed with four degree equivalents. This achievement surpassed the Gymkhana record at Jamalpur, which limited the attainment of degree equivalents to two.

Motivated by an additional incentive of Rs. five hundred for each extra degree equivalent beyond the mandatory mechanical, Lohani embarked on a race to set a record. His accomplishment led him to be recognised as the most diversely qualified engineer in India and possibly the world. Seeking further validation, he applied for a Limca record in 2007, which he successfully obtained. While publishers of *Guinness Book of World Records* congratulated him, they expressed regret in not certifying academic achievements.

This extraordinary start marked the beginning of Lohani's career, shattering any notions of being an average student. It was a testament to the power of one's mindset—the boundless skies of potential far outweighing the perceived limitations of life. Despite being an average student, Lohani's lofty dreams fuelled his journey to achievements, instilling in him the belief that he could conquer any exam, join any service and accomplish anything. The expectation of achievement propelled him to unparalleled heights as witnessed by the entire nation.

Hailing from the 1980s batch of Indian Railways Service Officers, Lohani is also a Fellow of the Institution of Engineers India and the Chartered Institute of Logistics and Transport.

In essence, Ashwani Lohani's journey showcases the transformative power of ambition, resilience and a mindset geared towards surpassing perceived limitations—a story that continues to inspire and resonate with individuals aiming for excellence.

Ashwani Lohani's illustrious career encompasses key roles in various prestigious organisations. He served as the Director of the National Rail Museum from 1993 to 1998 and later Director Tourism, Government of India. In 2001, he assumed the position of Chairman and Managing Director at the India Tourism Development Corporation until the end of 2002. Following this, Lohani held the role of Commissioner and Managing Director of the Madhya Pradesh Tourism Development Corporation for almost six years in three different tenures.

Transitioning to the railway sector, he served as the Divisional Railway Manager of the Delhi Division from 2009 to 2012. His journey continued with roles such as Chief Mechanical Engineer at Northern Railway and Chief Administrative Officer in the Ministry of Railways. In 2015, he took on the challenging role of Chairman and Managing Director of Air India.

In 2017, Lohani was appointed as the Chairman of the Railway Board, a position he held until February

"Dream big, persist relentlessly and in the pursuit of the extraordinary, ordinary becomes extraordinary."

2019. Demonstrating his exceptional leadership, he was reappointed as the Chairman and Managing Director of Air India in February 2019.

Throughout his remarkable career, Ashwani Lohani has been a beacon of values, achieving unparalleled success and garnering immense respect and love from those he worked with. His life story serves as an inspiration to many, with countless individuals attesting to the positive impact he has had on their lives. The recurring appointments to head prestigious institutions underscore his exceptional character, derived from a wealth of accumulated learning and experiences. In seeking to understand his journey, I engaged in numerous interactions with Lohani, unravelling the essence of leadership and greatness grounded in tangible actions and unwavering performance.

Contents

1
Record Unleashed

National Rail Museum

Ashwani Lohani had served in various capacities before he joined the National Rail Museum as the Director in November 1993. He didn't know why he was put in charge of the Rail Museum; the Director had little influence and the role wasn't prestigious. However, upon joining, he discovered the hidden possibilities. Working there until 1998, he turned things around remarkably, making his mark as a standout achievement in the story. Within four months of joining the Rail museum, he had an interview with BBC. This coverage gave the place worldwide recognition.

His first task was to get the Museum renamed from Rail Transport Museum to National Rail Museum which earned him national attention. The Museum rightfully got a place in the museum space of the world. Later, he set a Guinness World Record by restoring the 140-year-old locomotive named 'Fairy Queen' to its former glory. It was lying defunct and he decided to revive and run it. There were umpteen hiccups and snarls in getting this on track as it was old and discarded. He added luxury coaches to it and marketed this as heritage. He envisioned giving the passengers an experience of travelling with the oldest engine in the world.

His stint as Director, Rail Transport Museum, the so-called side-line posting has another success in his feather. During my meeting with him in Delhi, I requested Ashwani Lohani to share more about his experience of dealing with museums and the role as a curator!

When I first met him, I just listened to him for what he told me was so engrossing. What he shared with me is worth reading and knowing. "My affair with matters relating to heritage started with my appointment as the Director of the National Rail Museum, then known as Rail Transport Museum in November 1993. The shift to the museum in Delhi from the cosy confines of the Diesel Locomotive Works in Varanasi was precipitated by the arrival of a new boss who wanted to put me down just because I was the blue-eyed boy of the previous one. The new guy with focus clearly set on the stock market was hardly concerned about delivery at the plant and therefore, his rather biased assessment of officers on grounds other than merit," he said.

Ashwani Lohani travelled to Norway in 1995 to attend the annual congress of International Association of Transport Museums. Andrew Scott, the Director of the rail museum at York, personally took him around his museum widely regarded as the finest rail museum on the planet. He said, "Glistening artifacts effectively showcasing the history of the railway system in Great Britain, interesting authentic interpretation, well-stacked souvenir shops and an environment beyond comparison that attracted tourists in hordes was visible. The roundhouse in the centre of the museum where vintage steam locomotives were radially displayed was indeed the epicentre of the museum."

This meeting did something to him and he developed a deep desire to beat the York museum by setting a Guinness world record by reviving and running the 'Fairy Queen' of 1855 vintage, lying in Delhi. And so began the race for his first Guinness.

After returning from York, the very first thing he did was to give a good look to the 'Fairy Queen' that was then kept inside a building just outside the indoor gallery of the museum. Ashwani Lohani requested Dhasarathy, the then Executive Director, Traction, in the Railway Board for technical assessment. Dhasarathy was a steam buff. He said, "It was indeed his advice that was vital in deciding to go ahead with the project."

Excitement was in the air and creativity had started hitting the roof. It was decided that the 'Queen' would be resurrected and utilised to haul a two-coach train, a passenger chair-car coach and a service coach between Delhi Cantonment railway station and Alwar, a sleepy town in Rajasthan, almost a hundred and fifty kilometres away. The passenger coach would carry fifty passengers on a two-day one-night trip once- in-a-lifetime package on a train hauled by the oldest locomotive in the world. The package included a tiger safari and an overnight stay at the Sariska Wildlife Sanctuary. It was obvious that the 'Queen' had found a perfect partner in the tigers at the sanctuary.

"Optimism is not just an option; it's the only way forward. Pessimism kills effort and the will to try again and escaping it is our salvation from doom."

"Four issues had to be adeptly handled for making this dream come true. One was resurrecting the steam locomotive and making it mainline fit, second was finding two coaches and converting them into a service coach and a chair-car coach, third was finalising lodging, boarding and safari arrangements with the Sariska Wildlife Sanctuary and the fourth was printing and selling tickets along with all that goes in sales and marketing," he said.

He feels fortunate that the Board played a crucial role in the project's success, particularly by establishing an empowered committee. Bela Banerjee, the Executive Director for finance and Sudhir Malik, Executive Director for tourism in the Railway Board, were instrumental in his endeavours.

A two-day, single-night package was designed for the two-coach train. It was planned that the train would depart Delhi Cantonment railway station at 10 in the morning, reaching Alwar around 4 o'clock in the afternoon of 1 February, 1997 and leave on its return journey at around 4 o'clock in the afternoon of the second, returning to Delhi Cantonment at around 10 in the night.

From Alwar the guests would be taken to Hotel Sariska Palace, located in the Sariska Tiger Sanctuary around a 100kms away where they would spend the night and go for a morning safari. The trip was billed as a once-in-a-lifetime opportunity for 50 guests from around the world to travel in a train hauled by the oldest working steam locomotive in the world.

It was a grandiose dream for an officer of my seniority and vintage.

They received approval to run a special train hauled by the 'Fairy Queen', offering a package: a journey to Alwar on Saturday, the 1 February, 1996, continuing to Sariska for a night stay and a tiger safari, and returning on Sunday, the 2 February, 1996. The package, priced at Rs 25,000/-, covered train travel to Alwar, road journey to Sariska, all meals on board, stay at the hotel and a visit to the tiger sanctuary.

The difficulty he faced on a day-to-day basis was evident when he said, "Packaging this trip had not been a nightmare, as it should normally be, for the simple reason that the empowered committee route helped in quickly finalising the Hotel Sariska Palace at Sariska, Doon Caterers for on board services, printing tickets and collaterals, commission to the agents for selling the tickets, arrangements for coaling and watering at stations en route and basic improvements at Delhi Cantonment railway station and various other stations en route."

The field-level performance of the 'Fairy Queen' was not yet known as their assessment was based on many assumptions and theoretical constructs. But that is how most of the big projects of the world start. He said, "Our assessment about the speed, coal and water consumption and the stoppages required, it later emerged, were almost exact to the decimal. Perhaps it was the sheer intensity of my desire to run this train and in the process create a world record for the country that ensured the text-book success of this venture, ultimately after many setbacks."

His team brought full-page advertisements in the Delhi edition of *The Times of India* and the *Hindustan*

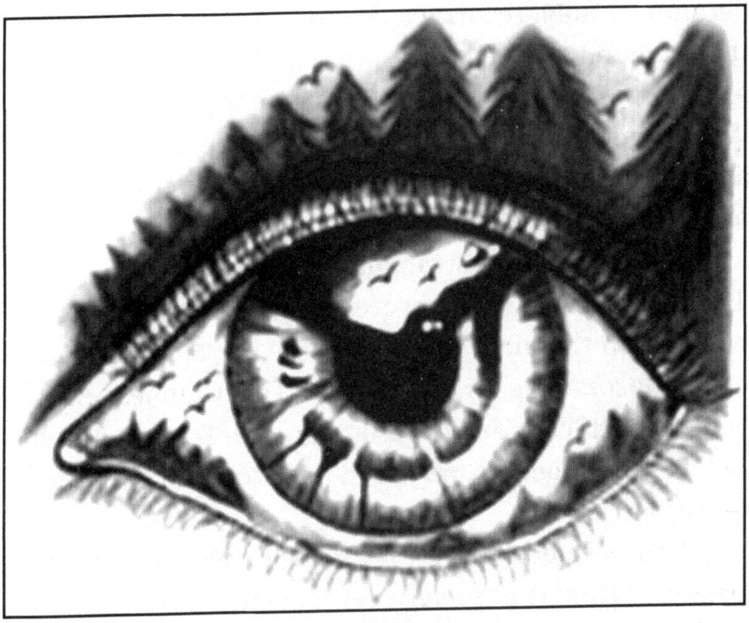

"Leaders envision greatness with eyes set on infinity and hands immersed in purposeful action."

Times. This was enough to attract everyone's attention towards his endeavour. "I got a dressing down for trying to build a hype by the bold advertisements, that too of a product that had still not been proven," he said. But the project continued.

Meanwhile, with great fanfare, sometime in September 1996, the 'Fairy Queen' returned from Perambur, fully resurrected and subsequently passed trial runs on the Rewari route. The trial run was done and the train was shown a green signal to go ahead. "Mike Woolridge of BBC was on the 'Fairy Queen' train with me and there were large crowds lined along the track almost all the way up to Alwar," he informed me.

The 'Queen' finally ran on the Alwar route on 17 and 18 October 1997. In the process it set a world record for running on the main line, hauled by the oldest working steam locomotive in the world. The Guinness world record certificate dated 13 January 1988 arrived much before audit queries and saved him from uncomfortable questions.

" 'Fairy Queen' train was for me a mission of extreme passion. I lived the 'Queen' every moment of my life, even in my dreams. My days were spent in her company. And therefore, almost every day I was late in reaching home and one midnight, my wife slammed the main door of the house in my face, asking me in the loudest voice possible to go and spend the night with the 'Queen'. In hindsight I realise it could not have been otherwise as it is only extreme passion in work that brings out the best in men and a price has to be paid either way," he said, full of passion.

The 'Fairy Queen' ran from Delhi to Alwar and back for about 50 passengers initially. He and his team of magicians put their heart into this, made it functional, aesthetic, beautiful, worked out a costing but the Ministry of Railways cancelled it. This came as a huge blow to the entire team and especially him. I could make out that we have a lot to learn from him. I reserved some of the questions in my mind and I wrote a few of them in my diary while I was making notes. He kept on speaking very emotionally; I just kept on listening uninterrupted.

Ashwani Lohani said, "The day of reckoning was only about a week away when I was ordered by the Secretary of the Railway Board to abandon this project due to very poor patronage. The ticket count remained at four on the day of reckoning and the project was abandoned. The 'Queen' that was parked at Delhi Cantonment railway station with its two accompanying coaches returned to the museum, dejected and in disgrace."

He was very emotional when he revealed to me, "And I wept and wept at the gate of the museum when the 'Queen' entered. Ojikutu, a German lady who worked at the German embassy and bought the first ticket of the 'Fairy Queen' also wept profusely. Together we wept till our tears dried. There were very few, almost none who could understand the pain I went through on experiencing my first major failure, although life later gave me many painful moments and also made me sturdy enough to accept both failures and success in their stride."

This setback couldn't deter Ashwani Lohani's spirit for long. Subsequently, after the 1 February 1997, the answering machine revealed many recorded calls of travellers who expressed interest in travelling on the 'Fairy Queen'. He recounts, "Were these expressions of interest taken to fruition, many more tickets would have been sold and the project may have succeeded." This thought implored him to again move a proposal for running the 'Queen'.

His aggression allowed him to have his way and this time the Railway Board not only agreed with his proposal, but also allowed him to launch the train at the International Tourism Bourse at Berlin in March 1997. He, along with his team, flew to Berlin, where they promoted the train and the concept of steam heritage tourism.

The spirits soared again. Days rolled by and the marketing efforts intensified. He said, "Commission to travel agents was increased and I personally called on every single ambassador in New Delhi, trying to sell my train to the expatriate crowd and also all major travel agents whose offices I personally visited in my drive to market the train."

13 August was the day of the first commemorative run of the 'Fairy Queen' express train. The trip had a couple of ambassadors, a few secretaries to the Government of India, railway officials and the mainline national and international media. Three days before this run, on the 10 August, during a yard trial, one of the axles of the 'Queen' had a hot bearing and the bearing had to be changed. Then one of the staff objected to its running for the want of few trials but Ashwani Lohani overruled him. He shares with excitement, "History was created the next day with my interview at Pataudi being carried on the

BBC breakfast news, the ultimate for any news story in the world. Newspapers and television channels splashed the photographs of this run and the image of the railways also soared high. Both me and Nathuram shared *samosas* that evening."

Now the 'Queen' was ready to run commercially but the Member Mechanical of the Railway Board issued a note cancelling the train trip on commercial grounds as only four tickets were sold. Ashwani Lohani shares, "I was devastated, yet not willing to give up. The previous setback had shattered me and a second setback would have been devastating. The dice had to be reversed and the opportunity knocked on the 12 October at the railway club, when Ravindra, Chairman of the Board, after looking at my downcast face, asked me what was wrong and I blurted out my sorrows almost in tears."

Lohani said further, "Ravindra was a sensitive person. He called me the next morning to his chamber where he had also called Sivakumaran, the Finance Commissioner. These two gentlemen had the grace and greatness to empathise with the pain of an officer almost 20 years their junior. On being asked what I wanted, I sought to reduce the price of tickets from Rs. 25,000 to a lower figure based on a marginal costing approach. The proposal and the resultant pricing of Rs. 6,000 was approved by the two gentlemen on the spot."

They approved the proposal to go ahead with the inaugural run on the 17 October despite having sold only four tickets, besides permitting Lohani to decide on the names of commercially important persons who could be

"Leaders uncover possibilities in the smallest things, achieving feats once deemed impossible."

carried on a complimentary basis. And these approvals were given by hand on a plain printing paper that Ravindra pulled out from his printer. He tells, "After all, Ravindra and Sivakumaran were leaders and not mere paper pushers that almost the entire lot of bureaucrats now appear to be."

Finally, he won. The first trip was a roaring success with tremendous international publicity; on the second, we sold 24 tickets; the third had 37 passengers; the fourth 45 and the fifth had a waiting list.

They tried with revised marginal costing and finally the dream turned to reality. It was a momentous occasion and he clearly remembers the name of the person – Ms Ojikutty from the German embassy – who bought the first ticket for this. Slowly, later, they got many more bookings and a place in the *Guinness Book of World Records!*

He happily shared, "The first pinnacle of success in my life had arrived. I filed for a Guinness world record sometime in the 1st week of November 1997. The media reports and the photographs of the run were sufficient for Guinness publishers, based out of London, not to raise even a single query on the veracity of the run. Finally, they issued the World Record Certificate on the 13 January, 1998, certifying the 'Fairy Queen' as the oldest working steam locomotive in the world with the certificate arriving at my residence on the evening of the 18 January, 1998."

A massive rush of adrenalin made Ashwani Lohani run to the Rail Bhawan to flaunt this achievement to the incumbent Chairman. Lohani barged into his room, all smiles and held the certificate for him to see, but, he gave the Guinness certificate a casual glance and said, "Okay, then." – merely 'Okay then' for setting a Guinness world record, not for growing fingernails or moustaches under the armpit, but for a real technological achievement of the nation. Sharing this incident, Lohani tells, "In that one moment I decided that from now on, my race shall be only for my own satisfaction; to hell with everyone else. I decided to keep the original Guinness Certificate at my residence. This interaction set the tone for the coming years in my life."

Persisting through setbacks and challenges, he continued with unwavering passion for his beliefs. Success, a hard-fought journey, didn't come effortlessly. Yet, he never wavered in pursuing his goals and dreams, emphasising the importance of chasing one's aspirations with every ounce of dedication and energy.

***

Ashwani Lohani detailed the story of transforming the museum from a neglected place to the centre of attraction – a spot many considered a loop line. "Director of the Rail Transport Museum was seen as a side-line posting and the incumbent was generally commiserated upon by colleagues. So was I on arrival at Delhi by everyone, including Sakkarwal, the principal private secretary of my direct boss, the Secretary of the Railway Board. Shaking his head, he expressed his sadness that I too would be wasting my time at the museum like all my predecessors without anything to show in the name of achievement. The challenge for me therefore was to some day earn appreciation from this

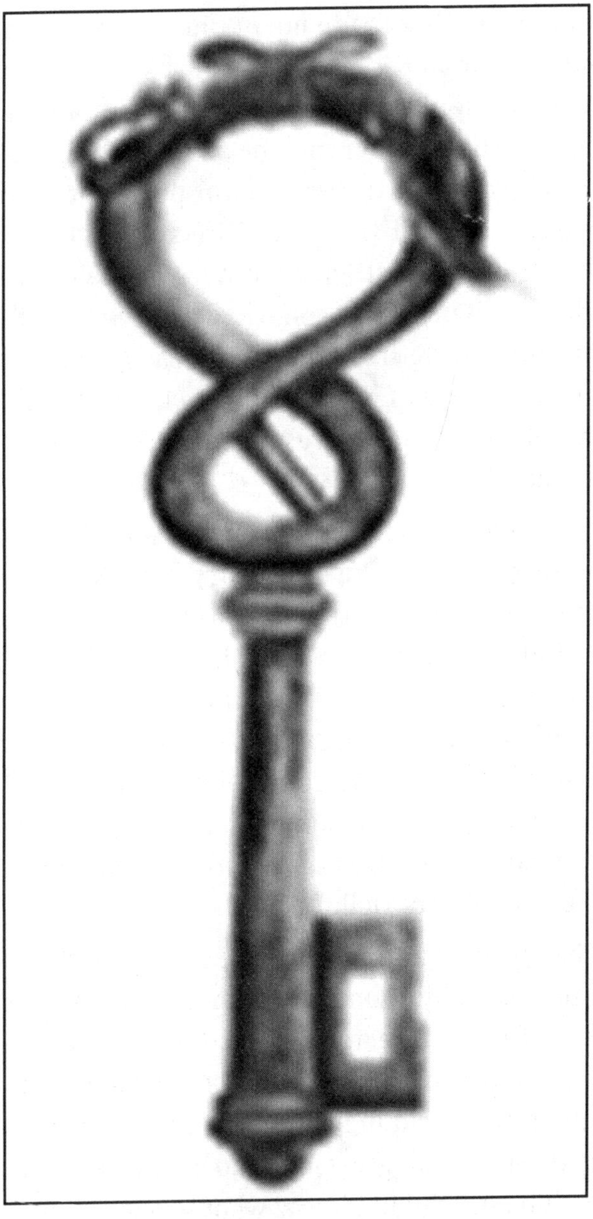

"Consistency is key. Never abandon your efforts. Where there is determination, there is always a path."

gentleman and that made me put in my best, right from day one," he said.

When he spoke candidly, it was a kind of revelation, "There is a sea of difference between staying busy and delivering, contrary to the general perception amongst the masses. Yes, till then, the Director of the National Rail Museum was neither busy, nor was he delivering. I intended to change the scenario. My five-year stint saw the museum rising from being an obscure place tucked away in a corner of Chanakyapuri to becoming the most vibrant and well-known museum and tourist place in the city of Delhi."

The museum with all its remarkable achievements including the revival of the 'Fairy Queen' and setting of a Guinness world record, bagging world heritage status for the Darjeeling Himalayan Railway, massive improvements in the museum infrastructure that included air-conditioning of the indoor gallery and building of a lounge and conference facilities and above all, positioning the museum as one of the finest rail museums in the world and a must-visit tourist attraction in the capital city of Delhi.

The museum attained an iconic status with accolades being heaped daily upon it by the media and the 'once side-lined' post of its Director emerged as the 'most wanted' post in Delhi. The staff of the museum could finally walk with their head held high and even Sakkarwal called him and said, "Well done, great job," and he was redeemed. "The lunch-club guys did not know what to say and my worthy seniors stopped advising me to look for another job."

The museum started participating regularly in the annual conference of the International Association of Transport Museums. For the first time ever, this association at his insistence decided to have its annual conference in Delhi in 1999. This was a very major achievement. The museum also became very active in the Museums Association of India and started playing a major role in the affairs of museums in the capital.

The museum had a fire engine from the days of the Nizam's Guaranteed State Railways. Built in 1918, this fire engine used to participate in heritage car rallies. They invited the team from Lallaguda workshops to revive this engine and participated in the 'Statesman Vintage Car Rally' in 1994 and won the Statesman Challenge Trophy. For the next five years, this engine won the trophy every year.

"My love for steam locomotives that was seeded at the Cawnpore railway station actually blossomed during my tenure at the museum. Formation of a society – Friends of the National Rail Museum – the first such society of its kind in the country that was ultimately amalgamated as the Indian Steam Railway Society was a memorable achievement," he said.

The stint at the museum gave him a Guinness record for running the oldest working steam locomotive in the world and also led him to file the first successful world heritage application for the railways – the Darjeeling Himalayan Railway to be followed by one for Mahabodhi temple in Bodh Gaya. This gave him the rare achievement of getting two world heritage sites encrypted for the nation.

"Opportunities abound in every corner, even in places without glamour. True performers can shine anywhere and everywhere."

Sometimes people feel lost when they do not get what they want or desire in life and get out of track. To succeed requires not only talent but qualities which make one persevere. In fact, it is this posting which anyone would consider a loop-line where he performed his best and showed to the world that a man can turn anything into gold just by touching it. Ashwani Lohani just worked while someone might just have mused in depression. It is this posting which established him as a brand – the turn-around man. He was picked up from here for his next posting and thus started his journey of turning around the organisations.

What he said to me shows what he feels about that posting now. By his own admission he shared it was a very special and interesting posting.

We see from this story of Lohani as to how one can find opportunity in adversity. Had he wept bitterly on getting posted in a place of insignificance, had he remained dumb by not doing anything as a protest against his insignificant posting, he might have landed in some neglected corners of Rail Bhawan eventually. But he chose to act; he chose to do something and do whatever he could to improve the place where he was posted.

That's the spirit needed for a person who wants to be successful in professional life for opportunity lies everywhere for those who look for them. And here is only darkness for all of them who just regret and repent. Things may not be as per our wish and satisfaction. To succeed in professional life is a big challenge as there are thousands of variables in the path. I feel the best one can do is to be honest in one's efforts. So what if people break your heart; you can still break records. Winners find opportunity in adversity and shine.

□

2
Triumphs from Challenges

Indian Tourism Development Corporation

When Ashwani Lohani was posted in ITDC, the corporation was being considered for disinvestment. He and his team thought that they would be able to turn around the story at Ashok Hotel and prevent disinvestment of the property. They were actually quite successful with the growth revenue of 66% but the story took a new turn when the property was up for privatisation. He very strongly believes that more than the shades of the organisation, heads of the organisation make a difference. The corporation had given the best financial performance a few years since he joined for the coveted property. The occupancy had significantly gone up; they were making continuous profits and the public opinion had changed drastically. The performance of ITDC was sterling at that time.

I asked Ashwani Lohani, "Please tell me about the biggest challenge faced in Indian Tourism Development Corporation?"

He said, "The biggest challenge was achieving financial turnaround in an environment overshadowed

"Strive for excellence, overcome challenges; a life without giving your best remains incomplete."

by disinvestment. The plethora of problems faced by the organisation was a culmination of years of lethargy, indecisiveness, political interference and unethical practices that the company allowed itself to be engulfed in. And the beginning, I was convinced, had to be made with the flagship Hotel Ashok in New Delhi. I soon inferred that what the organisation lacked was not resources or the market acceptability but leadership at the apex levels. So we focused on the flagship, its human resource and the need to be ethical and honest. And the men rose to the occasion. Unethical practices, indiscipline and corruption made a hasty exit and the finances started improving. The revenue growth in 2002-3 over the previous fiscal was over 60% despite my being given the boot three months before the end of the fiscal."

This is how he deals with the challenges. What he told me gave me the impression that running ITDC, the largest hospitality and tourism company of its time, provided a thrill of another kind. Competing against highly successful chains, like the Taj and ITC, that too in the aftermath of the 9/11 and in the process attempting to pull the company out of the abyss it found itself in, was an immense challenge.

The glamour of the hotels masked the poverty borne out of years of losses and the long faces of the men manning the desks in the company reflected the lack of focus on the human resource. Yet, the company, especially the iconic Ashok Hotel, slowly turned around despite being put on block and the downturn that the tourism sector had been witnessing in the aftermath of 9/11. To the chagrin of many, the men pulled the company out of the pits and started walking erect once again.

Turning around ITDC when it was getting disinvested was a huge challenge in many ways. The entire team who had zealously worked with him was low spirited, dejected and crestfallen that this was happening.

One employee of ITDC told, "It so happened once that the ITDC hotels were once put up for disinvestment and some private vendors were scheduled to take over. He spoke to us, boosted our morale, spoke to the minister, apprised him and explained to him how to get more funds, how to lease out spaces, how to explore more options for increasing the earning of the hotels. He actually became the architect of Ashok hotels."

One of the vendors of ITDC told me, "A new tourist destination was to be set up in Jharkhand. We wanted to be a major partner in this for event management and today, we are one of their leading partners. He took ITDC from 40 crores rupees in annual turnover to 100 crores rupees in less than five years. His mantras were – involve everyone in the growth story; no red tapism; he strictly followed the carrot-and-stick approach. During his tenure, pilferage went down. He set standards for everybody. He was the only CMD who actually got a farewell party and a standing ovation. We are still doing what he taught us 20 years ago."

Ashwani Lohani said, "I savoured the journey as much as the fruits of it. Despite treacherously long working hours, the tremendous love and affection showered by employees of almost all strata kept me going through. The most important learning during the journey has been that life is much bigger than everything else – a human soul is not to be wasted, discarded or pulled down. Getting the best out of your men is the only strategy that the top management should follow; rest the men would find out and implement. The established supremacy of the human resource needs to be recognised."

Ashwani and Vinod Kumar Duggal worked together in the Ministry of Tourism and Culture for about a year-and-a-half in 2001-02. While he was Chairman & Managing Director (CMD) of India Tourism Development Corporation (ITDC), Vinod Kumar Duggal was Director-General, Tourism and Ex-Officio Additional Secretary, Ministry of Tourism and Culture. He remembers his tenure with him as an amazing journey, full of challenges and major activities.

When I spoke to Vinod Kumar Duggal about Ashwani Lohani, he fondly told me, "One of the most striking memories I have of Ashwani is that the word 'no' did not exist in his dictionary. A very positive and result-oriented officer."

On the question about dealing with challenges, he shared one small incident. When they faced many challenging situations, Ashwani Lohani was always there to support and handle these situations. Lohani was the MD who organised the largest Pacific Asia Travel Association (PATA) Conference, in which over 1,000 delegates from all over the world participated and many other related major events were organised in Ashok Hotel during his tenure.

"Empowering teams turn disinvestment into standing ovation."

Vinod Kumar Duggal shared, "I would say that as incharge of this very important event, I was a bit nervous initially but Ashwani was always confident and indeed other senior officers like Amitabh Kant, Rajiv Talwar and late M.K. Khanna were also there to render full support. While I was concerned as to how we will handle India's largest tourism conference, Ashwani was very confident and would assure me with the words, 'Don't worry, Sir, we will take full care.'

He tells with confidence, "I won't be exaggerating if I add that it was the most well-organised and successful tourism event and earned a great name for our country the world over."

Vinod Kumar Duggal revealed about the disinvestment of ITDC, "This was also the time when Government of India had decided to disinvest some of the ITDC hotels all over the country. Although the ministry was the guiding factor and final decision-making body, the groundwork had to be undertaken by ITDC and Ashwani handled the whole thing in an absolutely transparent manner and not a single word of criticism was received, although several major properties were disinvested."

I asked Ashwani Lohani about his strategies and strength in dealing with ITDC under such pressing circumstances. He told me with full confidence, "'That impeccable integrity is the most powerful ingredient that any organisation aspiring for success should ingrain itself with. This was a thought that got reinforced repeatedly, with the realisation that integrity cannot be a strategy, but has to become a way of life for the organisation as a whole and also its constituents."

Lohani paused for a while and said, "I learnt that it is not merely bad decisions that kill organisations but indecision is the most powerful sure-and-silent killer. I realised that the morale of the men and the pride they have in the organisation is everything. And the inability of the top management to stand up for what is right and try to correct what is wrong, is invariably the biggest malaise that organisations generally face."

Vinod Kumar Duggal shared another story with me, "A most telling event that took place during this time and I recollect the bombing of Twin Towers in New York and also in some other areas in the USA which practically hugely damaged global tourism. What a coincidence that on 10th September, 2001, we had planned to have a Tourism Ministers' Conference to be chaired by Hon'ble Prime Minister, Shri Atal Bihari Vajpayee and both Ashwani and I were at Ashok Hotel, doing all the preparatory work on 9th September evening."

Vinod Kumar Duggal was sitting with Ashwani Lohani in one of the rooms, planning the whole thing when they saw live on television the terror attack happening. Duggal said, "It looked as if some movie was being screened. In reality, it was a case of live bombing of Twin Towers. We both immediately rushed to Vigyan Bhawan and I spoke to the Tourism Minister, late Shri Jagmohan as to what had happened. The Tourism Minister asked me to inform Hon'ble Deputy Prime Minister, Shri L.K. Advani, to brief him and take his orders. The Hon'ble Deputy Prime Minister, after being briefed, spoke to me for a while and asked us to inform all state governments that the Tourism Ministers'

Conference has been postponed."

The task was handled by Ashwani Lohani, Vinod Kumar Duggal and other senior officers in the ministry and the job was finished without creating any panic. Then, of course, to recover and rejuvenate the travel, tourism and hospitality industry in the country, the ministry took the initiative of branding the country as 'Incredible India' and marketing of this slogan worldwide was started in early 2002. Rathi Vinay Jha was the Secretary and Amitabh Kant was the Joint Secretary.

Kant took the responsibility upon his shoulders and was the driving force to ensure that the brand was marketed well throughout the world. Duggal told, "Ashwani and all of us were always there to help, assist and do whatever was expected. Rest is history about the super success of 'Incredible India'."

M.P. Bezbaruah, who was Secretary when Lohani was made the MD of ITDC, has a lot to say about him, "'He has acquired a great reputation for honest management style. I knew him in his formative years as a very young officer. He worked as my colleague in the Ministry of Tourism. He joined the Ministry of Tourism as Director when I was the Secretary. His name was in the panel of names given to us for the position of Director. His record was outstanding and we selected him even though there was some hesitation in some quarters as he was not from the IAS."

When I asked about Lohani's style of work , he told me, "I was impressed by his devotion to his work, his honesty, his capacity to work as a team and the ability to stand up for principles he believed in. Above all, he was

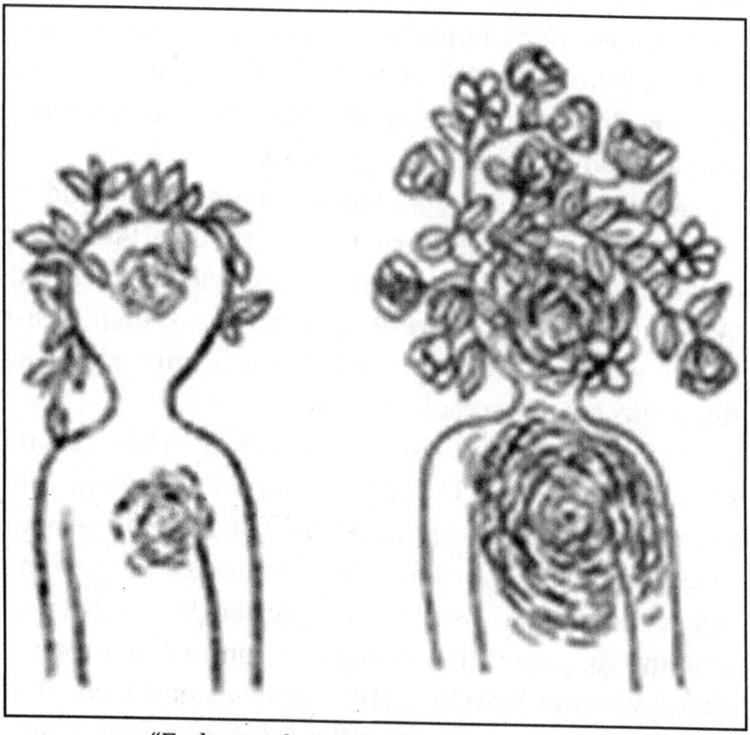

"Embrace change fearlessly, and let the courage within you redefine possibilities."

enthusiastic about doing something off the beaten track and his enthusiasm was contagious."

I asked Bezbaruah about a few things he did and he responded gleefully by saying, "I remember I had encouraged him in his innovative ideas and we did some spectacular things much ahead of time. Those days, because of some incidents, going up the Qutab Minar was banned. It was a great disappointment for tourists. Lohani created a virtual reality App which allowed the tourists the feeling of going up the Minar."

Bezbaruah continued with excitement, "Most tourists those days faced problems in selecting a reliable hotel and we had many stories of tourists being duped by unscrupulous dealers. For the facilities of tourists, we created an App of participating hotels and placed kiosks in airports of entry. Through this kiosk, the tourist could select the hotel of his choice as per budget, location, etc. and by pressing the link, he could directly talk to the hotel."

Bezbaruah cited another example, "Many tourists faced emergent situations like health, cheating, accidents, etc. and did not know where to go for help. Lohani came up with the idea of a one-stop call centre – the tourist had to dial a dedicated number to get assistance. This required coordination with different departments and I do not remember if the project did take off."

As he narrated these anecdotes, I realised that all these initiatives were taken up in the year 1998-99, much before technology and digital use had reached the penetration that it has now. From that point of view, he was much ahead of time. His contribution to the evolution of many things now being used commonly is indeed path-breaking. His deep interest in heritage tourism and in steam locomotives is well known. He had taken great interest in Darjeeling Himalayan Railways.

Bezbaruah excitedly said, "I could see how excited he was about running one of the oldest locomotives – the 'Fairy Queen'. If my memory serves me right, he had persuaded me to travel on it to Alwar. I shall never forget that journey. I was even allowed into the driver's seat of that exciting journey."

Bezbaruah also shared how Ashwani Lohani stood up to pressure even at the cost of his career. During his tenure as the Chairman, ITDC, disinvestment was very vigorously pursued by the government. ITDC and Hotel Ashok in particular were in the hot list. Once he approached M.P. Bezbaruah to say that the Disinvestment Ministry, as part of the disinvestment process, had drawn up hundreds of pages of assets and liabilities list and wanted his signature on the papers immediately to process the matter.

Ashwani Lohani wanted some time to scrutinise the papers before he put his signature, which the Disinvestment Ministry was not willing to grant. M.P. Bezbaruah said, "I thought his concern was very genuine and assured him that I would take up the matter. I did, personally, but I was surprised that the reaction of both the minister and the Secretary were vehement, almost implying that the CMD was intentionally creating a problem in a matter of national importance. I conveyed the reaction to Lohani and advised him that in the interest of his career, he may think of some ways to sort it out. He told me that he would stand by what is right and he did. I admired his courage."

"Think out of the box and solutions and successes will follow."

M.P. Bezbaruah, in the end, said, "I am very happy to see him grow to such stature and make a difference in whatever position he held. He stands out for personal simplicity, courtesy, humane approach and dignity that he upholds everything he does. I wish to see him in even higher positions of public service."

When I asked about his thirst for special and creative efforts, Ashwani Lohani told me, "The thirst for more world heritage sites under the belt became only stronger after the first success. As the Chairman of the India Tourism Development Corporation, I again piloted the application for encryption of the Mahabodhi Temple at Bodh Gaya as a world heritage site in June 2001. With help from Benoy Behl, the eminent art historian of the country, we filed the application and in a miraculous reversal of fate, the application was accepted after going through a round of rejections."

In December 2002, Ashwani Lohani had to leave ITDC. He was given no reason, no explanation whatsoever and was to be discharged with immediate effect. There was a tug of war at the highest level of the ministry but the one who had made up his mind was unyielding! Hence this stint came to an end.

When I asked Ashwani Lohani about feeling on leaving ITDC, he responded, "It has been a tremendous journey and now as it comes to a close, my head bows down to all my men who indeed made living itself worth the while." He further said, "There was not even an inkling of what would lay in store for me after I hung my boots. However, a mere 45 days after my final exit from the railways, I was back in what is often regarded by many as

"Challenge the status quo. To stand for what one believes in and what is right is the sign of a judicious man."

one of the hottest seats in India. While in the first stint, the mandate was revived that in the present is disposal, perhaps more because of the inevitability of it. An effort at revival energises the organisation and one at disposal drains it. There is therefore not much fun this time; yet what is mandated has to happen for the tremendous confidence imposed on me cannot be allowed to wither away."

Despite his superlative performance, he was removed and repatriated to railways – his parent department. He felt hurt, was discomforting and he felt bad. But all this was just for a day or two, as he decided that he won't give the right to anybody or to any organisation to make him feel him low; he therefore would start afresh at the new place of his posting.

He jokingly shared that his removal from ITDC was covered in General Knowledge books under the title of 'Famous Dismissals and Life Sackings'. The thought that people who are honest, upright and relentless have to sometimes face difficult circumstances brought him some comfort. Also this was one instance where instead of being rewarded, he was being treated just the opposite.

It was very much a setback but he told himself that such events should be considered very temporary and should not be carried forward for long in life. One swallow doesn't make a summer. Life cannot be judged by one episode or incident necessarily! Everything must be seen in totality and that's why he didn't mull much over this unfair treatment handed out to him. Such are the stories of great men who see light even in adversity; who see beyond the travails and focus on newer horizons!

"Embrace setbacks as stepping stones, for, in resilience, lies the power to turn adversity into triumph."

The chief of TAAI, Jyoti Mayal said, "In the government sector, officers are generally afraid of taking decisions but he did so fiercely. He never misused his power or position. He always paid for all his stuff, food and everything. How he behaved definitely left a mark as he was unknowingly setting examples and standards."

These values were keenly observed by people and these left an indelible impression. There was a major transformation in ITDC and every other place he joined. He is easily accessible, anybody can talk to him, advise him and seek an appointment. His biggest quality has been his connection with each and every person who has crossed paths with him – his ability to seek advice and then focus on the larger picture.

I remembered one learning I had during such times and something to remember forever in the field of work – '*karmanyawadhikaraste*'. A difficult feat for any person but then Ashwani Lohani isn't just 'any person'. The quality of perseverance helped him in sailing through such setbacks, to be prepared only for many more blockbuster successes.

I could make out one thing from this story I heard from him and from many other people about his performance in ITDC – that when one gets the opportunity, one shouldn't miss it. It is the only way a person can make impressions about his capabilities in the minds of people. People with reference might go long or might not, but people with hard work and dedication go a long way.

□

3
Innovation Unleashed

Madhya Pradesh Tourism Development Corporation

The failing state of affairs in the field of tourism in the state, in 2004, prompted Uma Bharti, the then Chief Minister of Madhya Pradesh to call Ashwani Lohani. The Chief Minister wanted to know whether he would be interested in taking up the challenges and do something about the huge losses staring at the MP Tourism Department. He heartily gave his consent as he is the one who loves to live with challenges. His tenure in Madhya Pradesh as Managing Director of Madhya Pradesh Tourism Development Corporation started in May 2004.

When I asked about Madhya Pradesh Tourism, he said, "The stint in the heart of 'Incredible India' was not work, but an affair, an emotional one at that. One tends to fall in love with the central Indian state of Madhya Pradesh that was indeed crafted by the gods with tourism in mind. Yet the infrastructure and image that my mind had at the time of my arrival was at wide variance with what perhaps was the intent of the gods, who, as some publicity campaigns loudly proclaimed, had ensconced themselves in the southern state of Kerala as their own country."

He landed in Bhopal with optimism and hope but he was shocked to see the office of the Corporation. The tourism office in the New Market area of the city to a dilapidated, run down, totally neglected, crumbling and unkempt building spoke to him about the condition of the department. Inside the building, a 60 square feet unkempt room, full of files, covered heavily with dust and almost no decent place to sit, welcomed him. Then he took a round of the entire office and every new room appeared dirtier than the previous one. The toilets were equally poorly maintained. He thought, 'So be it. Let us start from today itself,' he said to himself.

Since there was no proper room to sit, he called the staff for a lift lobby meeting, just outside the room. He instructed everybody that within the next 24 hours, it should be cleaned thoroughly and he would take a round at exactly 5:00 p.m. to oversee the progress. Such drills had mostly been a part of his tenure in more or less every organisation. No one expects the boss to be so active like that – that too on the very first day itself. Looking at the resolve with which he said, the staff started their cleaning spree, which, in turn, led to some decent clean rooms by the next morning.

Though the rooms were spic and span now, but they couldn't do much about the broken chairs, torn and tattered upholstery overnight. He summoned the engineer the next day and asked him to prepare an estimate for renovation. The engineer inspected the site and gave him an estimate of approximately 30 lakh rupees for the refurbishing work. However, the General Manager and the Chief Engineer informed him with no hope of a better future that since the department had been suffering huge losses amounting to Rs. 35-40 crores, no new things had been initiated over the past 35 years.

Lohani laughed it off, saying, "If the department had already incurred such huge losses, how did it matter if they spent a little more!" He put his point clear across the staff and told them that the office has to be redesigned. He asked the engineer about the time it would take to complete the renovation work. The engineer was so engulfed in his morose attitude that he answered with as much laxity as he could afford to, "It will take a minimum of six months or more for construction." Lohani ordered that within 30 days, he wanted a new office. They had no other option but to comply with the orders of the senior.

Chief Minister Uma Bharti called Lohani on the third day of his arrival in Bhopal. She wanted to inquire what he was doing and what he was planning to do ahead. He casually replied, "The very first thing I am required to do is improve the office! And even the establishment. Everything is in poor shape. I can't ask the staff to work without the basics. It should be done within a month."

Lohani established the office well and now started concentrating on Palash, which was one of the most important affordable hotels in the city. Palash had 33 rooms, one coffee shop, one conference room and one restaurant. A total strength of about 55 people worked to manage the hotel. The turnover of the hotel was somewhere around one crore rupees. But it needed a major overhaul. He started taking regular monthly

"True leaders possess vision and creativity, where innovation not only sets them apart but forges their distinctive brand."

reviews, meetings with officers, managers, housekeepers and everybody else, who had some contribution in its operations, to understand the dire state of affairs in the department.

After many such rounds of meetings, Lohani sat down to devise his own plan. By his assessments he forecasted that by October of the same year, he would be able to turn around the department decently. In just four months! Everyone else thought him to be running his own dream factory. Profits were not as much on his mind as getting a better balance sheet. He was being judicious with his thoughts and he expected to make a positive increase of 7-8% growth every month and about 50% increase by year end.

After reviewing the administrative structures, Lohani transferred about 60 managers. He issued the orders without any discussion with the ministers or obtaining their signatures. The transferred managers started getting their orders cancelled as they did not want to comply. He called a meeting of all these managers and tore the note sheets in front of them, to send out a message that the consequences of not following orders would be disastrous.

Later, Lohani also looked a little deeper for the reasons for which so much ruckus was created over the transfers. He found out that the houses for staff were in dilapidated conditions. They felt their families got disturbed when they had to shift; some had old parents who stayed with them and a few other reasons. So he came up with the idea of allotting houses to the staff, cars for all the manager-level staff along with a servant for all

"Learning is a continuous process. Learn with the challenges, learn with failures and learn with successes."

managers and above. He provided for an entertainment pass for all. He announced to his staff that he would provide them everything they wanted in return for more work and more revenue.

He understood very clearly that poor personnel management was leading to low morale of the employees. Thus they were not motivated to take ownership and perform their duties effectively. He saw the gaps, identified issues and resolved them; this certainly led to better results for the organisation.

Ajit, who worked as general manager in Palash, in Bhopal, said, "He improved the food services; started outdoor catering, packed food services. He introduced the wedding packages which were extremely profitable. During his time, Palash added suites, a party hall and two conference rooms. After he stepped in, the logistics were provided; hence the entire staff could work properly. He believed in delegation of powers and he announced to us that the General Manager of the property was the Managing Director and so he had to make decisions for his team. All headquarter- and regional-level governing and management issues would be under the purview of the General Manager. The security system became better, recoveries went down, pilferage went down and theft became non-existent. Now employees had no time to gossip or indulge in shallow power struggles."

I asked Ajit, "How did he deal with the belligerent staff?"

He replied, "He talked to everybody, took feedback from every person. He has a way of connecting with people and once he met them, they wanted to work harder. Soon there was a sea change in the attitude of the entire staff. He inspired us all." He further said, "The footfall at the hotel increased enormously and this was proof of the quality of services Hotel Palash started giving."

He improved the hotels at all the other places. For instance, Pachmarhi, which is a very beautiful place and a popular hill destination in Madhya Pradesh, had very few comfortable places to stay. He personally got the hotels redesigned, took care of the smallest thing which people generally tend to ignore. He made the staff learn by going to places and organised training for them. Ajit said, "He sent a team of some of us to Kochi and few other places for a site exposure to see and understand the boating facilities, so it could be replicated here in Madhya Pradesh."

Madhya Pradesh Tourism bears testimony to his quality of making quick decisions. His abilities to take quick decisions helped the organisation in tiding out the delays that happen because of non-clarity at the highest level.

***

When I asked about his family, Ashwani Lohani replied, "I have been indeed lucky in that. My better half, Arunima, has been the guiding force in my life and never allowed me to deviate from the right path. Taking advantage of the high positions I occupied with amazing regularity, it always remained out of the question. So when she made only one demand on me when I became the head honcho, I was not surprised, but immensely touched. She only asked me to set the NRCH (Northern Railway Central Hospital) right and obliquely threatened

"Don't procrastinate; be a quick decision maker."

me of consequences if the same did not happen in my tenure. Well, this is the power of the wives."

I asked about the work life balance, to which he replied, "I don't believe in the concept of work life balance. Life has to be led in a way that gives satisfaction without regrets. A totally ethical conduct and unwavering focus of delivery in the interest of the organisation where one is working is the best way to live. The balance thus arrived is the best balance that can be achieved."

By October, about Rs. 17-18 crore profit was made by the department for the first time! The next year, in 2005, Ashwani Lohani left for Delhi as he faced two challenges at the family front. First, his father was detected with cancer and second, his daughter was to appear for Board X exams. The growth during this period came to a standstill.

Vinod Kumar Duggal said, "Besides official work, a sterling quality that God has blessed Ashwani with is to be a perfect family man and a good friend to all his colleagues, be they junior or senior and be always helpful. An ever-smiling civil servant with his kind of panache is not seen that often. We have been in touch even after his and my retirement and I have no hesitation to say that one doesn't see a civil servant of his qualities that often."

Family has always been very important for him. He has never neglected his family for work. In fact, he has always maintained balance in all the aspects of his life. One of his friends told me, "Ashwani came to attend my daughter's wedding despite his utterly busy schedule."

Naresh Kapuria is a New Delhi-based painter, sculptor, installation artist, designer, producer and curator, who

"Strive for harmony in work, family, friends and relationships for a well-rounded life."

is a trend-setter in his field. His description of Ashwani Lohani overflows with the love and warmth he feels for the man. He is full of praise and only good words for him. He shared that Mr. Lohani was extremely helpful and that he has never met such a generous and wonderful person in his entire life. Naresh Kapuria worked with him during his posting in railways when he made a 120-feet painting and again when he made a 520-ft painting for Madhya Pradesh.

Hearing Naresh Kapuria was akin to hearing the applause one gets on winning some medal or award. After all, how many people command such respect? It comes only with work and nothing else. People may respect us on our face on some occasions, but the true test of that respect is when people speak the same good thing behind our back and all the time.

These words were echoing in my heart for quite a long time as I was remembering the talk I had with Kapuria and I was giving shape to my thoughts in the form of this diary. I felt being in the hearts of people is a greater reward than any other reward of the world.

I learned from this particular stint of Lohani that there is no limit to the creative energies one has. The only requirement is the effort to discover oneself, listen to people and be ready to learn at every point of time. Besides, the performance doesn't come with heavenly ideas but with simple actions. Our actions are more important than our expectations.

□

4
Learn from Spiders

Around the year 2006-07, Lohani returned to the Madhya Pradesh Tourism Department, after which the profits kept increasing very steeply. He believes the reasons for this turnaround was the high energy of the staff, their morale and the ownership they felt due to delegation of powers. The head of the department was the final decision-maker and no senior or minister had the power or say in the affairs of the corporation.

Later, Lohani got a new office building sanctioned as the old building was dilapidated, unkempt and he felt people had stopped thinking and ideating in that old structure. Nothing motivated them to work in that old building. He thought that probably with a change in location and surroundings, the staff would come up with better and fresher ideas. The intention behind all this was to have a motivated proactive team and increase the revenue and make more money.

Lohani got the new building inaugurated by the then Chief Minister during his second innings. The new building was located in a good location of Bhopal on Bhadbhada Road on about 35,000 square feet area. It is a beautiful structure, looking very impressive. The office still stands tall though it might have lost its past glory and lustre.

During an interaction, the chief of TAAI, Jyoti Mayal, said, "He's like a magician with a magic wand. He has the impeccable image of somebody who can turn around anything he touches. I wish there were more people like him."

Jyoti Mayal has known him for more than 30 years now. She shared that his vision for tourism was far superior. Lohani understood the importance of availability and ease of commuting, especially in the tourism sector. So he acquired the Volvo buses, which was a first for the state. He ensured that simple things, like cleanliness which mattered the most were not overlooked anywhere, at any location. He made sure these things were taken care of and emphasised this during all inspections.

Lohani specialised in turning things around within budgets, even with resource crunches! He travelled a lot, made numerous site visits and communicated with as many people as he could. He had the knack of understanding people, connecting at a level where they trusted him so much that they wanted to deliver, work and do better. He somehow saw the best in them and motivated them, invested in them to give their best and probably they saw his dedication which rubbed off on them.

It is true that when somebody trusts us, we want to do better. He is very comfortable with people as he makes them feel seen and heard. He values people and that always works in improving things significantly.

The then Chief Minister was so impressed with the

structure and his office that he even commented, "This office is much better than the CM's office." The Chief Minister looked at the white board in the office, on which Lohani had scribbled: 'June 30, 2008', and asked Lohani, "What is this date?"

He replied, "Sir this is the date when you would get the 'Best Tourism Award'." Hearing his reply, a big roar of cheer and laughter spread across the room. But his words proved to be true as Madhya Pradesh actually bagged the Best Tourism Award that year.

"Can you please tell me the challenges in Madhya Pradesh Tourism?"

"It was an organisation that was in the red since its inception and that cast an omnipresent shadow over all aspects of its operation. The morale of the staff was at its lowest ebb and shine was not to be seen in any of its establishments. The state of Madhya Pradesh, despite its unmatched richness of destinations, location, climate and law and order, was also not reckoned with in the field of tourism." He continued, "Reviving the tourism corporation, making it the best tourism corporation in the country and the state of Madhya Pradesh being acknowledged as the number one state in tourism in the country was the challenge."

"How did you deal with those challenges?"

"The challenge was taken head on. Treating the staff with compassion, empathy and care that comes naturally to me was the most important component of the turnaround mission. And giving them a vision of being the best run corporation, way better than the private sector and making Madhya Pradesh the number

"Success begins with strong teamwork. Those who collaborate and strive for collective victories are true winners."

one state in tourism, almost electrified them. Coupled with quick decision making, staff welfare measures and avoiding nitpicking, the blend was a recipe for sure shot success and, we were successful in a very big way."

He is a hands on person and he dived into work headlong with his team. He took care of every aspect diligently. He made a good team of engineers and architects and they all went everywhere together. He also looked into other areas of developing new sign-boards, installation of these signages and judiciously developing the *ghats* across the state. There was so much happening under his leadership simultaneously that one day a Sarpanch called him and requested, "Sir, *sadak bana do* (Sir, please construct the road for us)."

This tugged at his heart. He didn't know that his work was causing that kind of impact that the common man felt he was the one responsible for all developmental work on the ground! It definitely speaks about the kind of person he is and how he was turning the pages of the tourism department in Madhya Pradesh.

Another significant move which actually marked the state on the map of tourism was the creative design of campaigns to advertise the activities and facilities of the department during his tenure. He kept aside a separate budget of Rs. 2 crores and brought a new thinking that attracted the attention of the entire country and won international fame for Madhya Pradesh Tourism and brought the state on the global radar of tourism.

The first advertisement is remembered to this day for how it captured the essence of the state and highlighted the tourism sector in a unique way. He persuasively used television and radio for his campaigns which gave the tourism industry a 360-degree turn in the state. He kept on doing something or the other every new day and every next week of his tenure.

"Realising the difficulties in changing the place of lodging, we resolved to create a tourism eco-system that would enable the gods to take a holiday whenever they wished to. And so the heart of 'Incredible India' was born, with the state grabbing the bulk of national tourism awards since then. And again it was all and only about getting the best out of the men who manned tourism," he said.

This one time, while he was with Madhya Pradesh Tourism charges of corruption were levelled against him. He called up the MLA and stoically spoke down to him that he was very happy the MLA was fighting against unjust practices and he demanded a list of the frauds he had committed and asked him to be upfront about the charges.

Lohani has always been extremely upright and has a reputation for doing things the right way and never indulging in debauchery. This was a blemish on his name and he was seething! He called this man for 30 days continuously and every day to get a response out of him, but in vain. On the 31st day, he gave him a piece of his mind and lashed out at how dare he write or say something so defamatory about him. He could fight back like this because he has lived his entire life and career with utmost and absolute integrity which he feels has been an asset and he takes pride in living his life with rectitude and fairness.

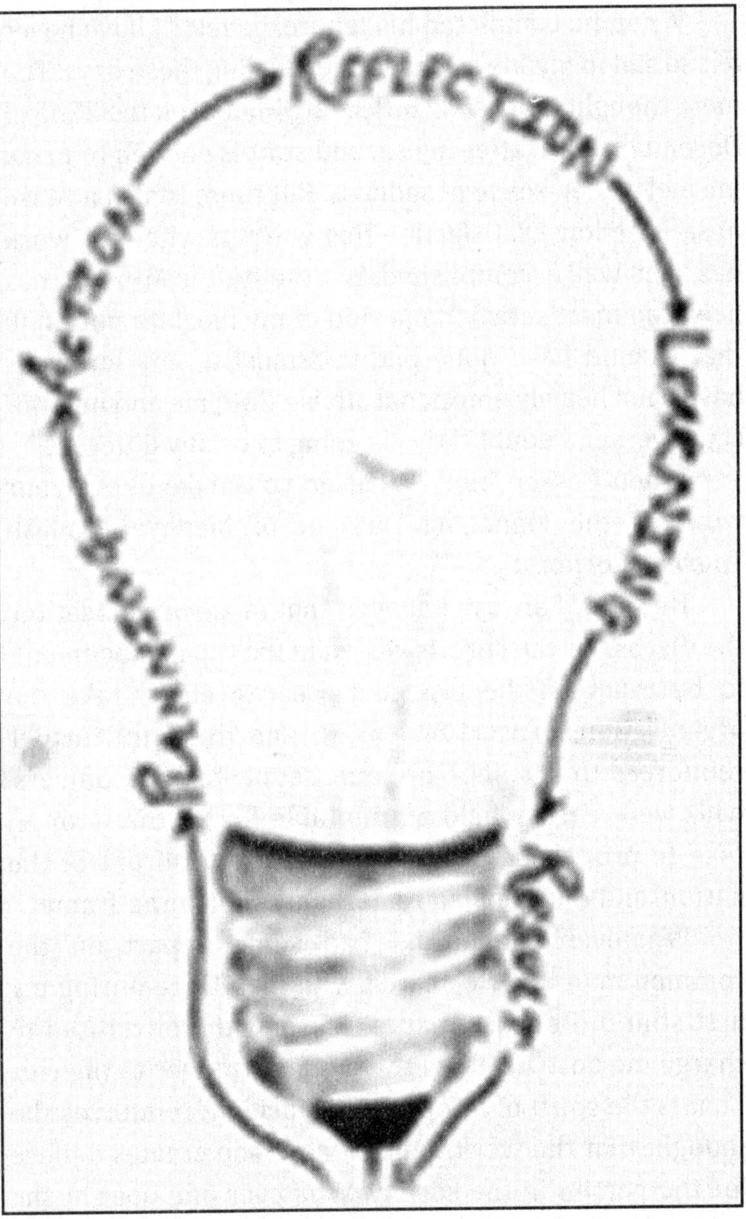

"Commitment reveals intentions.
Intentions set the stage for action."

When he completed his tenure, he felt, "I have never felt so sad in my life as I have been feeling these days. The mere thought that I shall be leaving Bhopal on the 22nd of December 2009 after my second stint is enough to make me feel a deep sense of sadness. But there is also a sense of satisfaction – satisfaction that one gets when the work has been well accomplished. Yes, the stint in MPSTDC has been the most satisfying period of my life. I do not think that I could have done better. Almost all my farewells have been heavily emotional affairs. Both me and my staff cry, together. I doubt if this is going to be any different."

When I asked him, "What do you make out of your work as the Managing Director of Madhya Pradesh Tourism Corporation?"

He said, "I always believed that in any organisation, the disease or the cure, is vested in the top management; to be exact, in the top man. He can either take the organisation forward or sink it. And this stint further reinforced this belief. The same set of staff and officers, who were earlier held accountable for all the wrongs, rose to propel the organisation to the forefront of the nation, and that too in a remarkably short time-frame.'

Whatever Lohani did had some impact on the common man too. He shared with me, "Once during my first stint in Bhopal, an auto-rickshaw driver refused to charge me once he knew that I am a stranger to the city. That is the spirit of Bhopal." This incident reinforces the thought that the work done by a person creates a place for the person in the society. Whatever one does at the helm of affairs does not matter if it doesn't touch the life of a common man.

"Dedication brings windfall rewards."

It is rare that one is posted back to the same position one holds. I remember the example of one of the founders of the widely-respected company Apple – Steve Jobs. Lohani was posted again in Madhya Pradesh Tourism as it was believed that he was bringing the change required in that organisation which has run some immensely creative campaigns to attract the tourist from across the world. Yet, when he was posted back, he didn't leave the opportunity to learn and deliver. The arrogance of success shouldn't blind a person to leave learning, while failures shouldn't deter people from learning again.

□

5
Positive Climate Change

Divisional Railway Manager

Delhi was preparing for the ensuing Commonwealth Games when he was posted back to Delhi. The speed reminded him of a humble man preparing his house for a brief visit of his wealthy friend. All areas that the foreigners may visit or see were either being spruced up, or being hidden.

Being recalled to Delhi, just in time for improving the railway infrastructure ahead of the Commonwealth Games was an honour as well as a challenge. Time was at a premium; funds were a severe constraint and the complexity of the procedures stood in the way.

He said, "'Yet, exciting it was to be pinned to a wall, when a quick sprint should have been the order of the day. And with the thought uppermost that success or failure is primarily a state of the mind, my team surged forward and did not disappoint.'"

On being asked about the immediate challenges in light of the Commonwealth Games, he responded, "I also have to get on with the job of improving the three major stations of the city in earnest. A monumental job no doubt, but possible. After all, it was in Delhi only where I got mine and also the railways its first Guinness by running the 'Fairy Queen' and also where I almost achieved the biggest turnaround of the country at the famous ITDC."

"Sir, you have worked in so many places; how do you compare Delhi with Bhopal?: I asked Lohani.

He responded, "Having lived for over 11 years in Delhi, I am definitely not an alien here. But Bhopal still feels more like home. Is it because of the artificiality of Delhi, or the crowds, or the dirt and dust, I can't say. But definitely, it has something to do with the genuineness of the people of Bhopal. Delhi is more commercial, even in matters relating to personal relations. Here one is assessed and treated more on the basis of how powerful or wealthy one is. Sometimes human values count much less here." He continued, "Yet here I am to do a job; a specific job assigned to me. It is no doubt more difficult than the job at Bhopal, yet the same shall be done. After all, sheer will power is still a much more potent force than many other powers."

Being a very positive man, he said, "As always, I was excited and was waiting for the non-stop excitement to begin."

When I spoke with Harbhajan Singh, who was the Chief Office Superintendent and also the leader of Railway Employee Association, All India Railway Federation in Northern Railways, he shared his sentiments about Lohani, "He had been working in Delhi for some time and it is one of the most important, biggest divisions of railways where approximately 43,000 workers are part of the staff. During Lohani's term, the Delhi division improved a lot. He had great ethics and an amazing and excellent level of delivery of work. Under his leadership, Delhi saw new designs, platform changes and newer designs."

Lohani shared the story of his days as DRM (Divisional Railway Manager), "I landed in Delhi on the 23rd day of December 2009. Yes forewarned I was, almost six months back that the mantle of Delhi would fall on me, not because of any special affection for me, but out of the administrative compulsion to make visible improvements in the main railway stations of the capital, ahead of the ensuing Commonwealth Games, lest railways come in for a flak. Administrative compulsion because railways was seen to be lacking in its efforts ahead of the Games, while other *sarkari* agencies had moved by leaps and bounds, perhaps inspired by unethical reasons that later surfaced. Why they chose me over many others is a mystery; yet, it appears that the sea of change that engulfed Madhya Pradesh in its tourism domain during my tenure may have triggered the selection."

I asked him, "How could you understand the Delhi railway station so well?"

He answered, "There was a two-room rest house for me on the third floor of the New Delhi railway station building where I parked myself for the next three months. This development, though unnerving for me, proved to be a blessing in disguise as it enabled me to understand both my boss as well as the ground reality at the premier railway station of the Indian Railways – it was a station that badly needed improvements ahead of the Commonwealth Games."

"Ethics – It's not a word but a habit. It's an attitude towards life. It shows the depth of the personality of a man."

Lohani further said, "I spent the entire day strolling around the station premises to get a feel of what actually awaited me as the most challenging component of my new assignment. I experienced the station in its totality – its dirt and grime, its crowds and chaos, its touts and coolies, its clients and its men."

When Lohani asked one person whose mandate it was to make the station clean about the state of affairs, he revealed, "I buy the brooms to keep the station clean." He said, "This one statement of a person wedded to the ground made me fully aware of the extent to which the system appeared to have deteriorated and the level of challenge that stared at my face."

In a challenging environment, he never considered himself as a boss. He was more like a guardian, mentor and friend to all those who formed a part of the team. He says, "On the very first day I promised, my team of senior officers, outstanding confidential reports and full liberty in the matter of travelling on duty or proceeding on leave and an absolutely transparent and accessible administration. They were also promised an administration based on trust, respect and value systems. The promises were solemn without any preconditions."

He added, "The focus for my entire term was going to be bringing about infrastructural and cultural changes in the division and this intent was laid threadbare on the table. I continued this practice of tabling my focus areas at all conceivable opportunities to avoid any lack of clarity in my team on issues I was going to pursue. The first interaction had a softening effect, yet the anticipation remained and rightly so, in tune with my belief that the proof of the pudding lay in eating and proclamations by politicians and officials should always be taken with a pinch of salt." He always trusted his team and the people around him. That made people reciprocate with efficiency.

Delhi is a large division, the largest on the railway system. This posed a bigger challenge for Lohani, in fact the challenges as DRM (Divisional Railway Manager) appeared to be bigger to him than any of the previous postings. For instance, no empowerment or delegation, a tremendous backlog of infrastructure, rampant corruption and a workforce that lacked motivation and was thus devoid of hope – the environment lacked enthusiasm and the battle could easily have been lost before it was even fought. Everyone thought he would fail.

There was over-supervision and over-control and the financial crunch and sustained lack of focus or direction were issues that defied handling. Merely focussing on the day-to-day operations and fire-fighting without any concern whatsoever for long-term planning ensured that almost everything was in tatters, be it the infrastructure required for passengers or that for the staff.

He says, "The biggest challenge before me was where I temporarily lived, the New Delhi railway station. And the Commonwealth Games were almost round the corner, a mere nine months away, a time-frame inadequate for even petty projects and restoration of the station did not fall under the petty category by even the wildest of imagination."

"Remaining focused is the recipe for success."

"How you dealt with those challenges?"

"I decided to walk, walk on my entire territory frequently and almost daily at the New Delhi railway station. With all concerned branch officers in tow, my inspections became a legend insofar as their frequency and regularity were concerned. The overall development plan and also every single issue was initially discussed threadbare in the chamber of the Station Manager followed by a long walk covering every nook and corner of the station," he said. He continued, "Initially I sensed reluctance on the part of a few of my officers on being pulled out of the confines of their homes on what they regarded as their day of rest, yet, with passage of time and with visible results started emerging on the horizon, the reluctance soon started fading away. There was almost always excitement in the air, non-stop excitement that kept adrenalin levels high."

Slowly and steadily things started falling in place all over the division. His officers started enjoying their new role of being change agents – change that had to be physical as well as cultural in nature.

There was one colony in New Delhi near Pandav Nagar where no employee was willing to go due to the illegal construction near Patel Nagar. The entire area was illegally occupied and had serious security threats which demotivated the employees for staying there. He immediately removed illegal structures, arranged for one pumping station. The entire area was turned around with a *pucca* boundary wall made for the colony. People live happily there without any threats now.

Ashwani Lohani also got new posts sanctioned for headquarters. He actually made the department workable. He was an excellent officer. He took the issues concerning his staff with utmost sincerity and issued orders using common sense, unlike other officers who made decisions irrespective of the required maturity for making sane decisions.

He told me something which I should share in his words, "Drinking within official premises was a major issue. Another was petty but widely practiced corruption even within the precincts of the divisional office. And the most shocking manifestation of the same was a section of the employees categorised as file-pushers seeking under the table compensation from the rest of the employees and also from all the contractors who worked for the division, for doing their rightful work – work for which the file-pushers were already getting salaries."

He has always been very concerned about the welfare of women and looked into their problems very sensitively. He said, "What really shocked me was the extent of sexual harassment of women, mostly the compassionate ground appointees who generally lacked a family support system. The situation was serious; rather, much more serious than what I had faced in all my earlier postings in the railways and elsewhere and made me realise that steps needed to be taken to rectify the situation at the earliest."

His long walks at railway stations, yards and staff colonies along with the extensive staff interactions helped to bridge the great divide and made the officer clan abreast of the ground realities. His management by

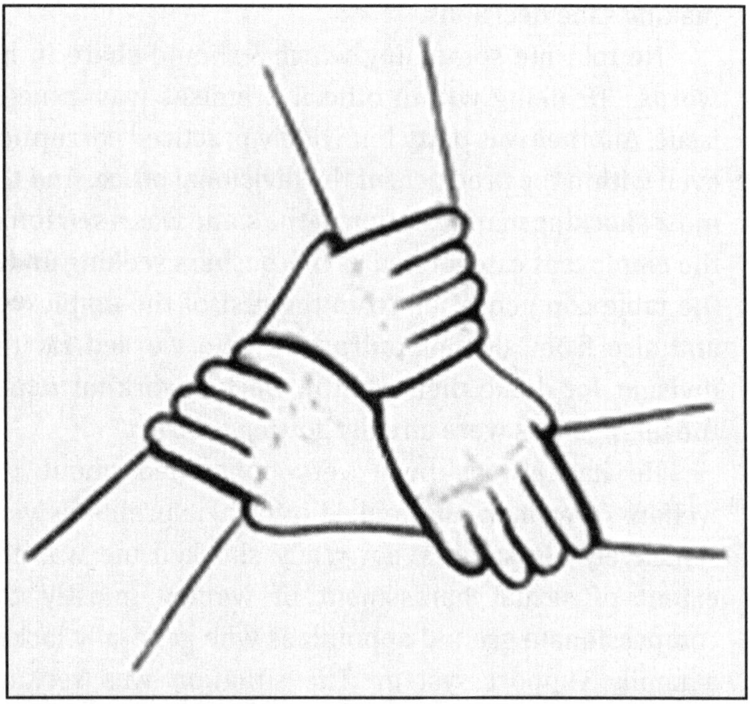

"Empathy is an invaluable asset and showing unconditional positive regard is a brilliant act."

walking around became a very popular tool to peep into the minds of the local functionaries.

Besides the walks, structured interactions with staff in large groups created an atmosphere of trust. He, along with his battery of officers, regularly interacted with the staff of all departments in large groups. Sometimes with office superintendents and sometimes with the personal assistants, *safaiwalas*, track-maintainers and the men who operate points to enable the trains to change tracks. It was the first time that such large-scale interactions took place.

Ashwani Lohani was astonished to see the positive changes it was bringing about. He shared, "During one interaction, an employee mentioned that he and others always noticed the Divisional Manager's car and it was for the first time now that they were seeing the guy in person and also talking to him."

His direct interactions with the staff grew with time and the opening of a central grievance cell ensured a strong redressal mechanism for all staff-related issues and in the process, bridging the divide even further. The staff of the division were free to call him on his mobile and also walk into his chamber for any problem they had. Though it was difficult to ensure the redressal of all the grievances, the mere fact that the staff had a direct line with the head of the division had a major and widely visible impact on the working environment and morale of the staff.

He told me about another initiative. "My quest for ground-level interaction was the conversion of an old second-class diesel-powered railcar into a top-of-the-line inspection vehicle replete with a pantry and a loo. They named this rail inspection car that became the pride of the division as 'Parakh'."

A unique feature of this car was the provision of separate television screens for each seat that ensured that the officers were well entertained while returning from an accident site or a gruelling inspection. He said, "The need to order a special train for formal inspections thereafter vanished. 'Parakh' also ensured swift movement of officers during accidents for it was almost like a personal car albeit with wheels that ran on the rail-track."

The introduction of 'Parakh' marked the beginning of creation of self-propelled inspection cars in the railways. He took another initiative to accelerate the speed of execution of work. He started regular interaction with the contractors of different shades. He told me, "We interacted separately with contractors from civil, commercial, mechanical, medical, electrical and other departments, generally every six months. The question, 'Whom are you forced to pay bribe to?' used to be the starting point of these interactions." The very fact that the head of the division and his two deputies had regular direct interaction, had to have a major impact on the way the organisation dealt with its contractors.

During these interactions, he repeatedly emphasised that a contractor was not merely a '*thekedar*' in the conventional sense but is more of a partner of the administration in ensuring delivery. The interaction with contractors helped reduce corruption to a large extent.

"Respect for all. Universal approach. The whole world is one."

Revival of New Delhi was a challenge greater than any that Lohani encountered earlier, for the revival was to be done with the station operations in full steam; not like hotels that one can close down and restore. And what a level of operations it was – over 500 thousand passengers passed through over 300 trains every day! That made doing anything almost impossible for fear of hampering operations always loomed large over our heads.

In his approach passengers' convenience was the supreme factor. He thought it necessary to avoid attempting to do everything and go about things in a focussed manner as funds were a serious constraint.

He said, "Decongesting the platforms, beautification of the frontage and shifting the parcels to a new shed on the Ajmeri Gate side was done really fast. The space released by shifting the parcels was converted to a large waiting hall replete with booking windows. The biggest advantage however accrued with the crowd being spread along the length of the platform, thereby ensuring an almost equitable usage of the three foot over-bridges and reducing, not eliminating, the perpetual threat of stampedes."

"Was your tenure smooth after that or were there some obstacles?"

"The unfortunate incident of a stampede at New Delhi station on the 16th of May 2010 taught many lessons and the exercise of ensuring uniform distribution of passengers on the three foot over-bridges had been a direct and an immediate fallout. While the stampede brought tremendous public focus on the railway station, it also led to slimy but unsuccessful attempts to unseat me from the hot seat. Yet the detractors failed and the juggernaut rolled on."

This gave him another reason to introspect, plan and ensure that the systems are put in place that makes it impossible for such adverse things to repeat. He said, "Rakesh was the chief architect of the transformation that happened at New Delhi and subsequently at the Old Delhi railway station. He carried with him his counterparts from other departments and that had been the one single factor that finally resulted in us winning accolades from the Comptroller & Auditor General of India. The CAG of India, in his audit report covering the Commonwealth Games, had praise for only one activity – that of the improvements carried out at New Delhi railway station and which were, in his opinion, carried out timely and within the prescribed budget."

He talked about cleanliness as well. How he improved cleanliness is a story in itself. "Direct interaction with the *safaiwalas* and appealing to their pride appeared to be the only way out. And therefore we had the first meeting with the *safaiwalas* of New Delhi station right on platform number one in the first week of March 2010."

It had a major impact with the cleaning staff (*safaiwalas*) undertaking a vow to put in their best effort for the sake of the image of the railways. Thereafter such interactions became a regular affair at all the three major stations of the capital and resulted in perceptible improvements all around. The contractors were also given full support and our efforts to bring in transparency in the entire system of managing contracts helped them to help railways in return.

He said, "'Our persistence paid off and the vastly improved cleanliness level was one major factor in the station qualifying for the national tourism award."

He feels it was the team spirit that was instrumental in the success he received during his tenure as DRM. He further tells, "It is necessary at this juncture to mention that our efforts to improve New Delhi station received national acclaim on three occasions, two of which were the conferment of National Tourism Awards in the category of most tourist-friendly railway station of the country."

These awards acted as a booster and reinforced his belief that sustained good work ultimately gets its due recognition. He said, "The biggest recognition for the New Delhi station however came from a totally unexpected quarter – the Comptroller and Auditor General of India, the CAG. While the CAG in its first report of January 2010 expressed its dismay at the alarmingly slow rate of progress, its inspectors had on subsequent occasions expressed surprise at what they felt were ridiculously low rates for execution of the works and also the fast pace of execution at New Delhi station. Their final report published in 2011, while taking the country by storm, appreciated the efforts of the railways in general with specific reference to the works carried out at New Delhi railway station for their timely completion within the assigned budget."

Naresh Kapuria called him an angel and an extremely upright and honest person. He shared with me that Lohani used to call him 'Nareshji' – and that was an honour for him. He was overflowing with praises for him and couldn't stop mentioning how humble a man Mr. Lohani is. Naresh is an artist and feels emotional about such things! He professed, "*Acchey aadmi hona ek baat hai aur kisi ko samaan dena doosri. Woh sabhi ka bahut hi zyada sammaan karte hain.*"

When I asked about the work at Delhi railway station, Lohani said, "Revival of Delhi came later, primarily because of two reasons – one, as there was no time for it prior to the Games and secondly, inadequate availability of funds. This oldest railway station of the capital was also the most deprived of the lot." He further said, "The station had a typical smell of its own – a smell that could emanate only out of shit that had caked between the tracks over decades. The station also had mounds of garbage stacked both at the main and second entry areas. Broken platforms, rotting infrastructure and an apology of the room that the Station Manager occupied were the salient features of this station that being a heritage structure should have been the pride of Delhi but was recognised more as the cesspool of the capital. A major task awaited us and therefore we wanted to look at Delhi only after the Games in New Delhi would have been almost over."

Carving out a proper second entry, rebuilding three island platforms and one end platform, improving the parcel area that was a prominent and major component of the station, creating a lounge for visitors, carving out a new post for the Railway Protection Force, building proper chambers for the station staff, clearing structures built in the yard and circulating areas over a period of time and which hampered visibility and maintenance were the works carried out in Delhi.

Encroachment was also an issue. They always removed heavy encroachments on Saturdays. There was invariably massive pressure from the representatives of the public and very often the drive failed on this count. In their mission they kept the channel of dialogue open and that led to the success of their campaign albeit not without push and pulls.

Lohani talked about the improvement done at the Hazrat Nizamuddin railway station. He described it thus: "Redesigning the circulating area at this station, refining the parcel infrastructure, relaying the main platform, creation of dignified work spaces for the station staff to work from, major improvements at the rest rooms for drivers and ticket collectors and marginal improvements at the second entry towards Sarai Kale Khan side were the main works done in a record time."

I said, "For me it is impossible to think of doing anything at these stations. How could you bring the change and the improvement we see today?"

"The recipe for quick success at these three stations was a suitable combination of frequent, almost daily field inspections, on-the-spot decision making, co-ordinated team effort by various departments, active involvement of the cutting edge supervisory staff and contractors and a target date, the sanctity of which was frequently broken without ruffling feathers but ultimately the tryst with what needed to happen was kept. Absolute integrity, both of the financial and professional variety, at all levels gave us the confidence and boldness that the corrupt and incompetent invariably lack. The brilliance, integrity and commitment of the dream team of officers of my division ensured that the recipe was properly cooked to completion. Overall it was a tremendous team effort and my role was primarily catalytic in nature. Just a catalyst, mostly a mentor and never a boss, that is how I view my role in all my postings, even in the ensuing ones," he explained in detail.

The overall environment needed improvement. The physical and the cultural environment had to be changed and for doing so single-minded focus and determination were required. He always focused on what was going wrong and kept on working in that direction. This focussed approach is one of the reasons behind his success.

Harbhajan Singh, the secretary of All India Railway Federation, said, "He visited the stations daily without a break and interacted with everybody. When he learnt that the DRM was responsible for everything but he had no financial powers, he made a presentation to the highest committee of Government Railway Board to ensure financial powers to the DRM since he was accountable for everybody but his hands were tied due to no monetary rights. This was accepted and the Board gave the financial powers to the General Manager. This was such a huge game changer for the railways."

Harbhajan Singh calls him an exceptional officer of India who brought down the losses of Air India and he is of the opinion that if the government had extended his tenure, he would have resurrected Air India.

Bringing about a cultural change is always absolutely essential, but for that to be initiated, it was necessary that the environmental changes should start getting visible.

"Leaders are the change-makers.
Prioritise, focus and be disciplined."

He did both by improving the drab committee room and other meeting rooms, thus laying the foundation for healthy and open discussion.

His coming down heavily people involved in sexual harassment, drinking on duty and corrupt practices with a sledge hammer did the trick and things started improving even on these fronts that were generally left untouched. Moreover, he and his officers were increasingly accessible. This improved the dignity of the people working with him and under him and boosted their morale. This coupled with the successful grievance mechanisms and the implicit trust he started reposing on his subordinates had a cascading effect.

The road on which the divisional office stood, the state entry road was also beautified with red sandstone on walls, paver tiles on footpath, cast-iron lamp posts and chain-link mesh all along for better access control along the track. And next came the turn of the rest houses, both for officers and the supervisors. Rest houses were also restored and made decent and comfortable and what really took the cake was conversion of two old coaches into a rest house for the staff.

Many such efforts to improve places and bring in efficiency helped him in turning around small places while increasing the satisfaction of the employees, for instance, the transformation of the steam locomotive shed at Rewari into one of the world's best.

For all his efforts he kept on getting awards. He could not recall the number of awards he has got so far. When I asked him, "Do you consider it luck that you succeeded on almost every task you took?"

He replied, "Luck follows the person who has the capacity to work hard with an attitude to never give up."

In May 2012, he moved out after finishing a tenure that gave him an unmatched experience.

Harbhajan Singh shared another anecdote of how he was enamoured with this man who worked 14-15 hours daily and whenever any issue was raised, he took it upon himself to find the best possible solution and deliver. Once Harbhajan Singh raised the matter of poor accommodation of railway employees. Lohani sanctioned the budget and improved everything.

Then another time when he saw that in the DRM office had no cabin for Harbhajan Singh, no air conditioning in the office that made the life of staff very difficult during the summer, Ashwani Lohani, as DRM, issued orders for renovation of the office. The entire office was soon air conditioned for the employees. Harbhajan Singhadded, "He was very sharp-witted and understood office politics clearly and so took decisions accordingly. In his 42 years of service and out of that about 25 spent in Delhi, he had never seen an officer work in the larger interests of his people. He is extremely honest."

Lohani recalledthe scene on the last day of his working as DRM, in his words:

The sound of drums and the murmur of the crowd gathered outside had almost reached a crescendo when I decided to walk out of my chamber in the late afternoon of the 15th of May 2012, my last working day as the Divisional Manager of the largest division of the national railway network. The impatient yet emotional crowd of railway men that numbered over 500 had a large sprinkling of the Pahari *people, who like me had their origins in the state of Uttarakhand. Garlands, music, dance and emotions flowed and I almost drowned, drowned in emotions that I knew would stay with me all my life.*

Despite the tears that flowed with amazing regularity whenever I moved out of all my postings, I never believed that even the dispassionate railways, that too in the heart of Delhi, can make me cry, but here I was, almost in tears, saddened by the parting with what was never mine. Love for what is never ours is the root cause of sorrow, yet some people like me never learn and should never learn. Perhaps it is all about being in love with the immediate environment, the animate and the inanimate; a love as pure as that of a mother and that is what makes this world beautiful for many.

It was only in the morning that I had witnessed an outburst of emotions and love from my men (and women) working in the divisional office. Almost every section in the office clamoured to bid me farewell, but for want of time only a few succeeded and what I got were bouquets of emotions and love. The official lunch-time farewell by the divisional officers continued past 4 in the evening with words coming straight from the heart. Only the previous day, the formidable Northern Railway Men's Union had organised a farewell, the first time in history for an outgoing Divisional Manager, and the three station managers of the major Delhi stations had organised farewell gatherings at their stations.

The zonal Association of Scheduled Castes and tribes also organised an emotional farewell in their office – a farewell that almost had me in tears and reinforced my belief in the goodness of men, irrespective of rank. The irrelevance of the artificial differences that rank and hierarchy in the government service create made a deep indelible impression on my psyche during the Association's farewell.

The round of office farewells ended with the warm send off by the Pahari *people, people of my clan, many of them necessarily not working with me, but associated with the Northern Railways. Even my car was decked up with flowers – flowers that reinforced in me the goodness of men almost everywhere. And as an officer I felt small – small at the pettiness of the officer clan in general that sometimes fails to treat their men as human beings. Our longing to occupy high chairs, not for the welfare of the organisation or its men, but for self-gratification of the petty kind made me feel small in front of this crowd of humanity that in one single moment reinforced in me the true meaning of compassion and humility.*

The number of 'full of hope' youngsters that I encountered during my Delhi stint gave me hope that all is not yet lost. A budding youngster told me that the railways is almost like the Chetak [horse] *of Rana Pratap that is just waiting for a hint from its master to gallop. Unfortunately, while we have a lot of blokes in the organisation and who occupy high chairs and corner offices, yet the number of those who have the capability to lead can be easily counted on fingertips, with a couple of fingers to spare.*

Lohani never relegated the personnel and staff management issues in the background as a low-key affair in comparison to the objectives of the organisation. This made people have immense faith in him and they gave their best through their work. It is a simple secret of managerial style that he practiced. It is not a strategy he follows, but he has a compulsion to work for the welfare of the people and keep the personnel issues above all other issues.

This humanitarian spirit makes him a leader with a human face and golden heart. This makes him not only successful but popular and a person anyone could trust.

□

6
Leadership Insights

Chairman, Railway Board

In 2017, accidents in railways were too many and so were the deaths due to them. Around July-August, there were too many accidents in the railways, too many deaths. Due to this concern, Ashwani Lohani was transferred to the railways. The first day he joined the office he was buoyantly received with about 50-60 bouquets and within the first hour of joining, he made three major decisions!

The most important decision that he made as soon as he joined the Railway Board as Chairman, wasrelated to safety. Yet there were many priorities. He made it clear that safety was going to be his first priority. There was emphasis on train operations but equal importance was not given to the maintenance activities.

Lohani made it clear that the trains won't run unless proper maintenance of all essential railway assets was carried out as per the requirements of safety protocols. This decision sent a clear message down the line that trains won't be run at the cost of safety. This was sufficient enough to gear the railway machinery to get to the task

"A true leader embodies vision, mission and genuine concern."

and ensure that accidents do not happen for want of maintenance.

The second decision he took was to reduce the paraphernalia of the office of Chairman. He started travelling with minimum staff and told them that he does not expect all the officers to throng the places he is going to visit. Rather only those officers should come who are required. This decision had the effect of setting professionalism in day-to-day working, thus paving the way for increased efficiencies.

Third decision which he took was that no one should bring flowers or gifts in offices.

He never considered himself to be the owner of the system and made his people understand that he is equally a public servant as them. The only difference is he is assigned the managerial role so that people have to listen to him but only for the things which are as per rules and has the sanction of the authority.

It is in this background that the tenure of Lohani becomes important and worth learning from. Many talented people leave the battleground at such a crucial juncture only to be lost in the pages of history. However, those who have the courage to take them head-on are remembered in the annals of history.

He hates frills by his own submission. He has never liked them and tried to eliminate them wherever he has been posted. He vehemently announced that firstly, no railway man will either present or receive bouquets. No person would assist in picking up the bag of Chairman as one could do that by himself; at the most, only one person will be allowed to accompany him for rounds, etc.

Secondly, no railway official would give or receive any gifts.

Thirdly, no protocols during visits; only the railway station master would accompany the senior; he would not allow a bevy of people to accompany the senior, only the relevant officials. These three decisions he made and announced within the first hour of joining. Diwali was around and he literally gave them a warning that he should see no cars and people flocking their colonies with gifts!

The biggest challenge for the railways at that time was safety and it was a major concern because of the prevailing situation at that time. Mr. Lohani feels that generally people in departments feel everything is a priority, which actually defeats the meaning of priority. He is of the opinion that one should be very clear with one's priorities. When one thinks that every single thing is a priority, then nothing gets done. One cannot have 10 priorities – something has to be top of the list! That's not how one can decide what is urgent and important. Clarity trumps every decision which will ever be made. He always worked like that and probably this was one of the many reasons he is who he is and has been able to achieve what he has.

He reciprocated this concern of safety when we discussed railways: "The immediate challenge was accidents; a spate of accidents that had taken place in the preceding year and were a matter of serious concern. Challenge was also the sagging morale, especially in the officer community and living up to the expectations that my arrival on the scene led to."

He recalls his railway posting and tells, "The ground connection of the management is the single most important factor that can make the difference between failure and success. My stint as the head of railways was gratifying because perhaps for the first time in history, the officer cadre of its own volition started moving extensively on the ground and in the process interacting with the field staff. Popularly known as '*samvad*', such interactions slowly became commonplace with even senior officers from the headquarters and the Railway Board visiting divisional headquarters, workshops, stations, depots and sheds and even the ones that were located in the back of the beyond. And for the first time gangmen, TTE's, *khalasis*, station masters, supervisors and staff of various other categories started feeling that their voice is important enough to be heard by those who matter. And the officialdom started realising that merely sucking up to seniors is not important; what is important is to know your own men, the men who are responsible to keep the wheels moving."

Ashwani Lohani told about the strategies followed by him, "The action was multipronged. First was building morale in the team, motivating them and giving them a purpose much bigger than merely their assignment. This was achieved by following an open-door policy, meeting and interacting with all my men, over 14 lakh of them, on an equal footing and telling them what is expected of them. It was also very important to lay down priorities without any ambiguity and I was nimble footed in clarifying on the second day of my joining that safety is the topmost priority and operations come next, not the other way round. This announcement played a crucial role in the rapid reduction in the number of accidents."

His weekly official inspections of workplaces in the divisions, specially the sparsely visited ones, evoked considerable enthusiasm, anticipation and also fear – fear for those who avoided their own men and therefore were not aware of the ground realities or those who were embroiled in unethical practices. The impact of such interactions was widely visible in the rapidly improving environment and the smiles on the faces of the men. It also helped in softening the feudal divide that had earlier existed.

"And therefore, 'samvad', the dialogue between the senior management and the field-level workers began with focus on the ticket collectors, who for the first time felt the warmth of the concern for the men on the field. During all my field visits, I made it a point to have a dialogue with the ticket collectors, talk to them without the local satraps being present and visit their running rooms. My inspection car had a big framed calendar, not of the railways but of the Ticket Collectors' Association and when I visited their annual conference in the Talkatora Stadium, the tremendous applause had me almost in tears," he said.

He paid great attention to the plight of the men who maintain the track. The silent unsung heroes of the railways who walk on the tracks in extreme heat, the biting cold and the slushy monsoons, performing their duties under extremely tough working conditions are indeed the mascot of the tenacity of railway men at large.

The men, who unfortunately frequently get run over on the tracks they maintain by the trains that run on them, deserve our ultimate respect and honour. These men who are literally attached to the ground and rarely have any clue of even their personal entitlements like provident fund and leave balance depend upon the mercy of the local *babu* for everything they should get. With concern for them, he revealed, "The official apathy and their misuse at the bungalow of supervisors and officers is really extremely sad." He ensured dignity for them. He heard them, improved their working conditions and physical facilities like toilets, rest rooms and resolved their personnel matters.

In fact to share their problems, he decided to walk on track and took a foot inspection on 15 December, 2017, on a wintery night. This is how he not only realised what this most crucial category of railway men goes through but also gave them silent assurance that the highest official of their organisation understands their grievance and problems.

Lohani did not leave any section or place or office where he didn't pay attention. He didn't leave the canteen even from his sharp eyes. Only to ensure that such a place also needed improvement and he got that done to the satisfaction of his staff. Thus, sending a message again that he cares. He did what had to be done. The canteen along with the conference halls, toilets, sections and the entry foyers, all improved substantially. This change in the environment did a lot to improve the general way of working in the Rail Bhawan.

Lohani has a unique way of reaching his office every day. He said, "I rarely went straight to my own ivory tower. Normally my entry to my chamber was preceded by a visit to a section or the chamber of a young officer who did not know how to react to the Chairman, who surprisingly just walked into his room to say 'hello'. A few words that revealed a lot and then straight to the ivory tower, but my day as well as the day of the youngster whom I barged into was made." He further said, "More than the morning visits, it was the organised rounds of the Rail Bhawan, rounds lasting almost two hours that gave me an insight into the physical and environmental inadequacies in the Rail Bhawan. Strange have been its inhabitants who talked about improving railways, yet did nothing about the apex headquarters, the building from where the mighty railway system is governed. And I am yet to be able to lay my finger on the cause, whether it was a mere ground dis-connect or rank apathy towards anything other than self-gratification or both. Perhaps it was both."

When one does so much for people, one gets respect in return. Such respect is greater than all the awards of the world. He shared emotionally, "Almost three weeks into my superannuation, a group of over a dozen gang men, staff who maintain the tracks, came to see me at my residence. They presented me with a spinning wheel, the '*charkha*' of Gandhiji as a token of the love and affection of over three hundred and fifty thousand men that they said they represent. They also said that it was only in my tenure that this category of staff was recognised and given the honour due to an employee of railways. Literally in tears, this group of men continuously thanked me and also implored me to continue to take care of the men who man the railways."

It has always been like this. His men were always in tears when he left them, for he loved them and they loved him. It has never been any other way for him. He addressed them as '*aap*' and never as '*tu*'.

Wherever he went, he was greeted with love and affection never seen before. They left no stone unturned to display their agony and despair whenever he left after completing the tenure. This was because he had taken great care of the personnel matters of the staff. He said, "My men caught hold of me when they wanted to and no place was taboo for the same, be it my residence, office porch, my chamber or the place where I was going for inspection. There was never any distance between my men and me, for I always believed that an assignment or a job is merely a role and does not confer a higher status on some roles vis-a-vis another." He always considered all the employees equal to himself.

On being asked about his strength and inspiration at the workplace, Lohani said, "I always keep a big national flag and a copy of the *Bhagavad Gita* in my chamber to help create an environment of pious and noble thoughts. While *Bhagavad Gita* ensures purity of thought, the national flag gives a feeling of pride to the occupant of the room and also the visitors."

He has always ensured the dignity of women at the workplace. He was moved by the work done by women in railways as it involved great physical efforts to get the work done. He said, "They perform jobs that in other

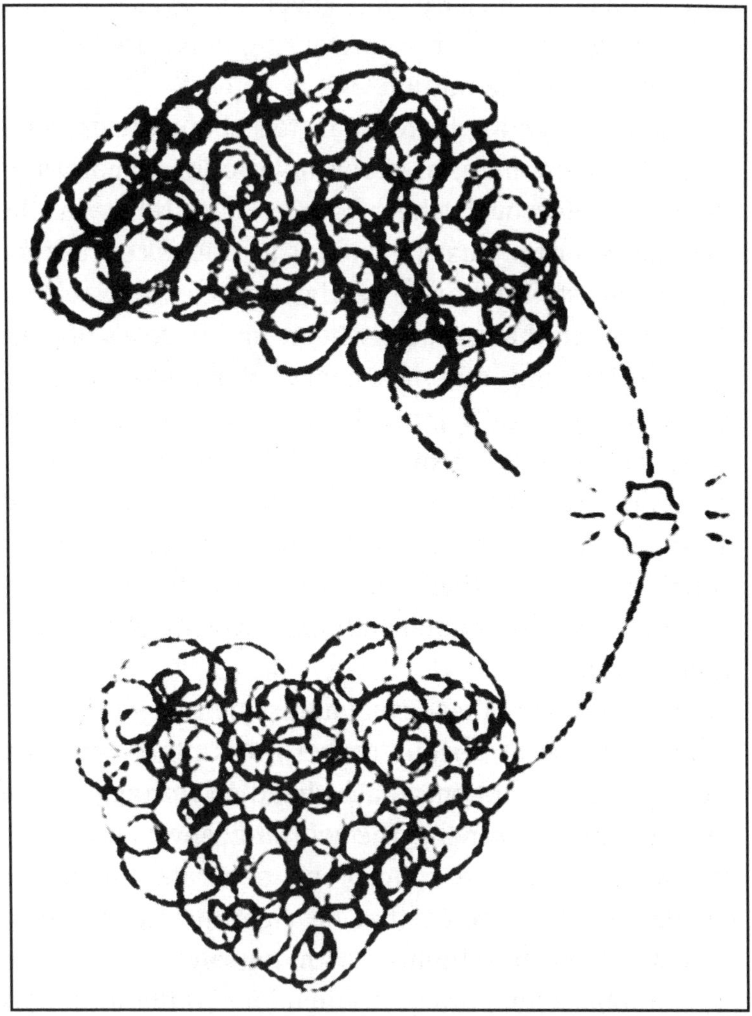

"Success in management thrives on empathy, compassion and emotional intelligence."

sectors, even men would shy from. Working as a loco pilot, guard or gang men is not an easy job for women, not only because of the hard work involved but also because of the risks involved in solo working in isolated places, often away from habitation."

He continued with pride to tell about them, "They stand the risk of harassment or molestation by notorious elements. Moreover, the absence of a toilet in the locomotive or the guard's cabin is a serious concern for the female staff, who unlike the males cannot release themselves in the open anywhere. And in cases of gang men, lifting and carrying heavy items like concrete sleepers is generally much beyond the capacity of the fairer sex, who are also at risk in isolated sections. It is keeping the safety of the female staff in mind that we recommended to the Department of Personnel and Training to reserve these three categories for males only. Yet the work that women staff do is worthy of our deep appreciation."

He was aware that sexual harassment in work areas is also a cause of serious concern. His office regularly received such complaints that he handled with aggression and aplomb. Improving the working environment by provision of change rooms and separate toilets for females was something that he vigorously pursued at almost all establishments. With improved sensitivity, even though temporary, tremendous difference was made in the working environment for females.

Ashwani Lohani told me an interesting anecdote, "Around a week before hanging my boots, a group of around 20 gang women, one from each of the zonal railways, along with a few office-bearers of gang men associations called on me. This group spoke about the difficulties they faced while discharging their responsibilities, primarily due to physical limitations on account of being a woman. They also highlighted the problems they faced due to laborious work, especially during pregnancy and monthly menstrual cycle."

While it was not possible to solve all their issues at one go, he advised Zonal Railway General Managers to issue instructions to post gang women in groups at yards only, provide change rooms and toilets for them and generally display sensitivity towards their genuine concerns. They went away fairly satisfied and so was Ashwani Lohani at the very fact that a group of staff from the lowest rung could call on the highest authority in the railways and freely interact with him was a sure sign of change.

He made full use of the technology and social media tools to increase his efficiency at work. One such application is WhatsApp, which is considered to be a very powerful managerial tool. With such tools he created a system that enabled his messages to trickle down to the last employee on the field, all in the course of a day. And the men therefore knew first-hand the desire of the top guy. He said, "Knowing what the boss wants has remained the biggest mystery in organisations and therefore employees fumble in attempting to please the boss, for they are always left guessing what the boss wants. The system of cascading WhatsApp groups that we had created ensured transparency and clarity regarding management goals and objectives."

Wherever he went, he has regarded the employees as an essential pillar of success of the organisation in getting the objective met. He has always been very empathetic to their needs and that has always paid him back.

Gone are the days of management when managers used to say, "I don't give a damn to anything other than work." He rather believes, "It has been my experience that at the human level, everyone is the same. It is the same human being everywhere with the same basic instincts and craving for recognition and always ready to be proud of the organisation he works for provided he finds reasons for the same."

Often many of us at the apex levels of management talk about lofty ideals especially for the staff at the lower levels, without generally believing in or following the same ourselves. At that time we fail to appreciate that even a concern regarded as small by the higher ups is big insofar as the lower levels are concerned. Merely the receptiveness of the management is enough to build confidence and pride in the employees. A kind word from the chief executive is a very powerful option for building up morale. Empathy at the level of middle and senior management goes a long way in organisation building, yet the same is generally conspicuous by its absence.

"Perform or perish" is an oft-touted slogan in many organisations, touted by the senior management and at the staff in general. He said, "I hate to hear it for invariably the ills of organisations are created and perpetuated by the top management, yet the blame is always directed at the men at large." He continues and says, "I long for the day when we in management would really appreciate the huge potential of the human resource and start taking steps to get the best out of our men."

Sometimes he walked with them, sometimes he played with them, sometimes he went to their colonies and offices, sometimes he ate with them and some other times he just listened to their plight and the result is for all of us to see. He succeeded in whatever he wanted to do.

Transformations are all about radically changing the way the organisation has been operating, thinking, treating its clients and its own men and above all, its perceived image. A successful transformation unleashes the hidden potential of organisations and enables them to achieve what was hitherto considered unattainable.

It is all about creating an environment wherein the people get encouraged from within to deliver their best. It is also about creating an environment where it is easy to do things, where the processes are simple and based less on the written word and more on mutual trust. It is about dignity, conduct, integrity and cleanliness and orderliness. It is about creating an 'utopia' on the ground.

Contrary to popular belief, transformations are simple yet highly passionate efforts. It is only passion and love for your men that can see transformations though, of course, peppered with a lot of common sense.

He told me about what he thought of transformation, "'Having tasted transformations in almost all the organisations that I headed, I was confident from day one, yet needed to find the starting point. With massive organisations like the railways that are inundated with issues and problems touching almost every aspect of the organisation, for any head honcho brimming with the desire to bring about a change, the biggest difficulty lies in identifying where to begin. The majority of the blokes unfortunately pass their entire tenure in waiting for the right moment and the right issue to surface while the organisation continues to remain where it is."

Ashwani Lohani brought those changes in the organisation which no other officer could think of. He had a deep understanding of working in government organisations that led him to initiate change. He talks of bringing about cultural reforms, which he did in his own way. Every organisation has a culture that evolves over a period of time and is invariably the reason behind the success or failure of the organisation.

The culture decides whether the organisation is sycophantic or meritocratic, whether it regards human value systems, whether it treats its own men with respect, whether its men take pride in working for the organisation, whether it inspires respect or fear in its men and so on and so forth.

He shared about his joining as Chairman Railway Board (CRB), "Receiving over a hundred bouquets within two hours of taking over as the head honcho convinced me of a serious cultural flaw in the working of the railways. That the organisation is feudal and also sycophantic was evident and to me there appeared a serious need to give a cultural jolt to the organisation and its men."

He further added, "Within an hour, a notice was put on the door of my room saying 'No bouquets, no gifts', and a curt WhatsApp message sent to all General Managers ensured that the practice of bouquets and gifts came to a screeching halt."[4]

And the next on his list of avoidables was protocol. He issued an order stating that the Station Master shall be the seniormost official providing protocol services to receive him did the trick and the battery of officials who used to arrive for receiving CRB just vanished. His one of the most talked about and the difficult action was the withdrawal of unauthorised staff working as domestic help at the residences of senior supervisors and staff.

He kept on reforming the processes in the organisation to make them more simple and easy for officers to work and convenient for the common man to understand and get services delivered easily. He believes in continuous improvement by continuously working on identifying the gaps and plugging them and bringing about reforms in day-to-day work.

Over a period of time, the multiplicity of verticals has ensured that even simple processes have become over-complicated. This is perhaps because of the way railways is structured with eight different services of the union manning as many verticals with the result that often the bureaucracy takes a myopic view, not a holistic one of the organisation. Simplification of the processes in railways was therefore a major focus area, for that alone would enable speeding up the up-gradation as well as addition of infrastructure that the organisation has been crying for since long.

Every organisation has processes for doing things. A large organisation like the railways would have tens of

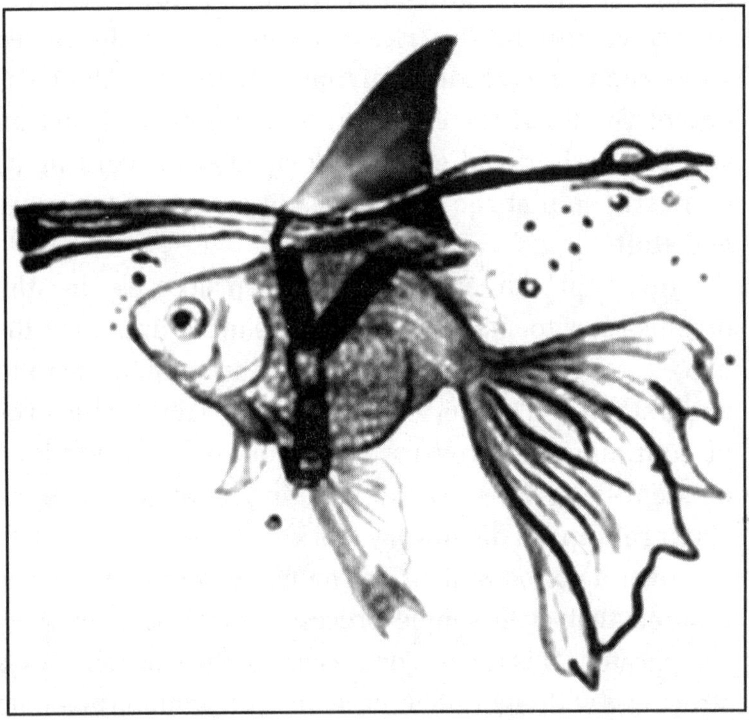

"Right conduct is of paramount importance in public life. Trust is an asset. Self-confidence is like a lighthouse. It guides when all other sources are waning."

thousands of processes for doing various things under the sun. And the realisation that deliverance, not the process, is supreme is unfortunately missing. And therefore, over the years, we have been flogging the system rather than trying to make it more efficient. Therein lies an unintended real tragedy.

Once he went on inspection to Ghaziabad to see the station. He reached and met the local officers. After the pleasantries were exchanged and the small briefing, they got tea, *samosa*, cake, etc. He asked them from where they got the money for this as they did not have any imprest amount or provision for such expenditure. It was understood that the contractor must have been asked to bear the expenditure for this. He made it clear to the staff that from next time, nothing except tea should be served and he would not allow such arm twisting of contractors, etc. for tea and food arrangements. Such practices promote corruption and he had zero tolerance to misconduct.

He firmly believes that it is the human resource of any organisation which drives the force. They should be valued and when valued, they take moral stands. He also actually believes in the saying that we are all puppets and are here for a short while to do our work. He also exceptionally thinks that all of us are equal and nobody is superior or above any other person despite our designations. We are all human before our titles.

He told further, "Lack of empowerment has been a perpetual issue with the railways and we tackled it on the front foot. Large-scale delegation of powers and simplification of procedures followed in the right earnest and a record over two hundred and fifty empowering circulars were issued in my tenure. This empowerment played a major role in enhancing the speed of improving infrastructure related to passenger amenities and staff welfare."

He concluded by saying, "That we should avoid frills and focus only on delivery was also made very clear right from the first day. On the day of my joining, we banned bouquets over the entire railway network, banned gifts and curtailed protocol to the bare minimum. We also looked down upon extravagant parties in the officers' clubs and the practice of utilising railway staff for petty household chores. And it had an impact. Officers and men started focusing more on their work that they also started enjoying."

During Ashwani Lohani's tenure as CRB, over two hundred circulars delegating powers on decision making, contractual and establishment matters were issued in the year ending 31st December 2019 and released in the form of a transformation booklet. Thus, deliverance had started taking a front seat.

To take swift and important decisions and make some palpable changes, for his first meeting he called the chief track engineers and instructed them clearly that "unsafe *gadi nahi chahiye*". He had a lengthy serious discussion with them and wanted all risky and perilous trains to go. Safety was supreme!

He analysed the problem and found that they ran too many trains and the maintenance was being compromised. Operations were taking priority over maintenance, hence the accidents were happening. He announced that from now on, safety and maintenance would be above operations. For the first time in the railways this became a priority.

He travelled extensively, all over India, to decrepit places, trying to cover all stations. He left office on Thursday or Friday evening and the entire weekend he was somewhere in India, meeting hordes of people in thousands, the station staff, guards, track layers, everybody. He met the operating staff, housekeeping staff and everybody as much as he could. He shook hands with them, patted their backs and thus made them feel a part of the same group, while they shied away from him in their sweaty work-clothes, hands and bodies soiled in grease or dirt. He met them and always asked what they needed.

His message to all was plain and simple as he generally said when he met them, "*Sab acche se chalao... jaan laga ke kaam karo...izzat ka sawal hai!*"

He categorically declared that he wanted safety, he wanted cleanliness, he wanted their dedication to shine through their work. He genuinely believed that people are always ready to do what you ask of them provided you let them know, ask and appreciate their hard work.

Lohani had zero tolerance for corruption and he made it clear that he would not allow that at any cost. Because he put a restraint on this, nobody misused their power to create ruckus. All hooliganism came to a standstill, but the clause still remains that it is possible only if one has a scrupulous reputation and zero tolerance to fraud and dishonesty.

He has a different opinion on how he likes to approach the government machinery and his position.

His firm opinion is that one should think like workers of the government, not like owners. He said, "The people in the government sector are there to work and should not nurse corruption."

Lohani shared about an interesting incident when he joined. He called the peon sitting outside and told him clearly that both of them were servants to the government. He said, "One sits on a stool outside, the other on a chair inside. Both of them can be removed from their position at any time. Anybody can be better, so nobody has to think they are higher than the people they are here to serve." It was matter for a hearty laugh and I'm sure the peon was shell-shocked on hearing this. I wish more officers would think like him. It is his unshakable belief that if the staff is with you, you can accomplish what not.

I asked, "'Have you ever felt that you couldn't achieve desirable goals? How did you cope with it?"

He replied, "It happened only once when my pet project of 'Fairy Queen' could not take off due to inadequate ticket sales and the apathy of the Railway Board. Yes I wept openly but again took up the cudgels and ensured that the 'Fairy Queen' ran not once, but five times during the next year."

Full of confidence, he further said, "I have always coped with setbacks and they have only been temporary, by rebounding with renewed vigour to achieve the targets set by me for myself."'

***

His support for the staff has been unparalleled. In the year 2018, on the eve of Dussehra, in Amritsar, one train ran over more than 75 people who were sitting on the track to see the Dussehra function to be held. The driver was not prepared for such an event and he had no information about the event. The crowd wanted to kill the driver and destroy the trains.

At such a time, he visited the site and declared two things – one was that the Railway Board was not responsible for this and he would not take action against the railway employees. Generally, after any accident, inquiry is set up and some or the other employee is temporarily suspended or an inquiry is set up. In this case, he announced neither will there be an inquiry nor will anybody be suspended.

Any other Chairman must have suspended the loco pilot. But Lohani had the conviction after knowing all the facts and circumstances not to take any action against the train staff. He believed it was not their fault. In fact the local administration must have taken care of this. This had a great effect on the morale of the employees. This is not the only such incident when he supported the staff whenever they were not at fault. This had won him the kind of respect and command that no previous Chairman must have felt.

It is beyond imagination what kind of a message he was trying to send amongst the 14 lakh employees of the railway! He stood his ground for both the declarations and the driver was provided police protection too!

***

When Swachh Bharat Mission was launched and Param Shivam was the secretary, Mr. Lohani called him to Nizamuddin railway station and they cleaned the station together with the housekeeping staff. After that, they came to platform number one where the staff

"Leaders exhibit courage in upholding what is right with a judicious approach."

had gathered and had tea and *samosas* with them. They were aghast how, after cleaning human waste with them at the station, these two seniormost officers were sitting with them and relishing food when every other officer would upturn their noses even at the stench of this waste. It was beyond their comprehension how this was even possible.

Lohani felt it was important to connect with everybody and people, if they feel seen and heard, always put in their best. This paid off. People heard about it as it was much discussed and talked about and eventually resulted in all stations becoming cleaner. It appears unbelievable but this is what happened.

He shared his feelings as a railway man, "Every class one officer who joins the railways dreams of heading it, but not everyone does for there is only one chair at the top. Returning to the railways in August 2017 as the Chairman of the Railway Board for a stint that lasted slightly over 16 months was like a dream realised. Despite brevity, the tenure was enjoyable for me and perhaps also for the entire team of much more than a million. Despite handicaps – departmentalism, infatuation with frills and complexity of processes – the tenure turned out to be an exciting one."

He continued full of emotions, "Being born as a railway man and being aware of all its follies, the mission was to set the railways right, but can one really do so in the limited time-frame available was the moot question. Were 16 months enough for setting right the world's largest organisation with a culture inculcated over 17 decades and the answer apparently is a big 'no'.

And therein lies the tragedy of railways. All its top-level appointments have generally been for only around a year and with the complexity of procedures and the sheer size of the organisation, seeing an idea from fruition to reality in the short tenures become difficult to say the least. All efforts die at the halfway mark when the guy who mooted the idea passes into oblivion."

□

7
Sky is not the Limit

Air India

Air India was indeed the toughest nut to crack, not because of the toughness of the nut casing but because of the huge debt it piled up during its attempted nosedive into oblivion – a dive that could be successfully yet temporarily halted by bringing out the best of its men and also its machines. And at the root of the dive was always a management that was as distant from the ground as the moon is to the sun.

Some bad decisions of the past that are already in the public domain – the stark absence of a ground connection and decision-making processes that would put to shame even the word 'complexity', together conspired to pull down an organisation that in the past ruled the skies with impunity.

In August 2017, he left the glory of the skies, convinced that the airline still has in itself a lot that could propel it to emerge as the leader that it had always been till a decade back, provided the handicaps that it is saddled with are shown the door.

He felt, "The ill-famed merger of Air India and Indian

Airlines, even though on a much smaller scale was a disaster, the after effects of which are still being felt. It also needs appreciation that departments and the cadres that man them are two entirely different things and clarity is required whether we need to merge one or both. In any case however, railways being a highly technical edifice, we would need to retain specialisations or in other words, departments and this needs to be suitably addressed. The issue is delicate and we need to tread with adequate caution and care and also remember that mergers are complicated exercises that take time and need highly effective management to properly handle the associated change."

When I asked about the most challenging task of the career, he said, "It is difficult to pinpoint one task as most challenging. All my postings posed challenges that cannot by any stretch of imagination be classified as trivial."

He continued, "The biggest challenge was obviously the turnaround of the national carrier 'Air India' that overshadowed even the challenge posed by the largest organisation on the planet, the Indian Railways. And the almost impossible challenge was so because of the huge debt that the airline had piled up since the ill-fated merger of 2005. The debt was almost Rs. 50,000 crore when I landed in the cockpit, in August 2015. Huge debt entailed massive debt-servicing costs, almost to the tune of Rs. 4-5,000 crores every year – that was partly met by equity infusion by the government and partly by further loans taken by the company against government guarantees. We were in a vicious bind and that was an impossible challenge. I knew that while this impossible challenge cannot be overcome, it would be good if the airline could be turned around operationally at an EBITDA [EarningsBefore Interest, Taxes, Depreciation and Amortisation] level. And the operational turnaround happened during the year 2015-16, delivering the first operational profit since the ill-fated merger and yes, I can accept that we partly failed in meeting the real challenge."

Lohani told further, "Another challenge was to energise the staff in an organisation that was in losses since merger, was suffering from major staff-related grievances as a consequence of merger. Almost everyone had a burning grievance, had an ivory-tower management style, was grappling with serious financial issues and had major industrial relation problems."

"How did you manage those challenges to achieve success?"

"The challenge was met by following a totally open style of management, being on the floor, meeting men, interacting with them, apprising them of issues, talking about ground realities and being totally positive, allowing not even a shred of negativity near me. And the icing on the cake was that we did not hesitate in even banning a ruling coalition Member of Parliament when he manhandled a field-level employee of Air India. The morale was high and if the morale is high, can success be lagging behind?"

He continued, "Quick decision making, not procrastinating also played its role. Within three months of my joining, the world's longest commercial flight was launched between Delhi and San Francisco. This one flight that was in the works for more than four to five years did much to lift the sagging morale of the organisation and new international flights started getting launched regularly. Besides San Francisco and Washington in the United States, we connected Vienna, Madrid, Stockholm, Copenhagen, Tel Aviv, Nairobi and Birmingham as also launching additional frequencies to Australia, Dubai, UK and USA. Induction of additional A 321 aircraft on lease enabled dozens of new domestic flights. All these new flights brought in a lot of energy into the organisation apart from revenues."

Another Air India officer, Jagannath, the Chief Executive Officer shared his fond memories of Lohani. He remembers the time and cherishes the work done with him. He categorically mentioned, "Mr. Lohani went out of his way to find workers' issues and solve them. He was a very bold decision maker. A few international flights were not taking off, so he set them up. He launched them in a big way. He first assessed the situation, then worked around a vision and opened several stations which other Managing Directors could not. He took sharp decisions without vacillating. He made decisions which others could not."

Most CMD's never meddle or bother with the political parties but he was not one to shy away from fierce, firm decisiveness. He said, "One of the politicians misbehaved with a cabin crew and he put the politician on a 'no fly' list to protect his staff and send out a message for the power-drunk megalomaniacs! There was tremendous pressure but it didn't bother him an iota; he stood with his staff."

He would regularly engage with the staff at all times. He roamed around the terminal, discussed problems and solved most of them. He even frequented the integrated centre for flight control, sitting there, listening to everybody's arguments and then making the best decisions for the larger good. He always looked at the bigger picture! He was very fair, listened to each and every department, analysed every aspect and then arbitrated. Every department had numerous things to say. He was approachable, so people automatically opened up to him.

He couldn't fix everything but he did his best to come up with the finest solutions possible. He even put up drawings on walls, flat names and numbers for the staff houses, arranged Independence Day gatherings and everything that promoted the camaraderie.

Meenakshi Malik joined Air India as a management trainee and then took charge as Director (Commercial) in June 2020. She worked with Ashwani Lohani and shared some insights into his working style. She shared that the first time she saw him briefly was when Rohit Nandan was leaving and Lohani was taking over as Chairman.

Seven days after he took over, he called Meenakshi Malik. In her mind she thought, 'Okay, another Chairman, another head making nothing much of it. There was some parliamentary question and he needed to send in the reply.' When she reached him, Ashwani Lohani asked, "Can we sell the aircraft?" in light of the crisis Air India was going through at that time. To this, she replied, "No, not of course."

He immediately asked her, "Prepare a note why we should not do that."

She said, "Pankaj Shrivastav, who was the then Director, was also against it but Mr. Lohani still went ahead with it. He was firm in his decision and he always made fast decisions. He listened to people. He wasn't high handed or short sighted. He was very respectful, good with people and his priority was always people."

She got impressed with his working style and immediately started assisting him in whatever way she could. She said, "He would sit with us and analyse flights and show keen interest in every aspect. He sat with the staff in their offices, engaged with them while they worked and listened intently to everybody. When he saw the shabby working conditions, he ordered new computers, got everything cleaned up, renovated the entire area and improved the sitting arrangements. He complained how we were working in such squalid conditions. He got the Civil Works Department to clean it up for us which made working conditions better. His primary concern was always his staff and he wanted to provide the best possible solutions for improving their productivity which definitely goes a long way in any organisation, but few people look at these obvious things at senior positions."

Jyoti Mayal feels he is a great leader who is always willing to take ideas from every person, engage in talks with them and then also communicate the outcomes with them. He shared his decisions liberally with the employees, unlike other government officers.

One example of how well he connected with everybody was that once, on her visit, a junior loader at Air India fondly mentioned that he missed 'Ashwani sir'. Such was his enigma and presence that each and every person missed working with him. And to have such reverence towards a senior in the government sector doesn't come easily and every day!

Another extraordinary quality he had was that he never met people by introducing himself as the Chairman of or as the head. He used his name and not with his position which mostly government officers do to inject a sense of fear and intimidation amongst their colleagues and juniors. He was always humble, open, supportive. He wrote everything with a lot of clarity – he was a swift decision maker. A very astute and sharp man with incredible brains!

***

On several occasions, when Vinay Sanan, Lohani's childhood friend was travelling and whenever he mentioned that he grew up with Ashwani Lohani or they are friends, the behaviour of people around suddenly changed from indifference to utmost respect and love. He says, "If Ashwani knew that I was travelling, suddenly help would arrive from nowhere for some assistance." He shared one incident, "Once in 2007, I was travelling in 'Shatabdi', going to Jhansi from Delhi. I just mentioned to the staff that this change in Delhi station was brought about by my friend Ashwani and I was awestruck by the respect I received from the railway staff. "It was not due to his position or fear but because of utmost respect for Mr. Lohani," he continued. He realised that Ashwani Lohani must have done something exceptional that made the staff respect him in his absence.

He tells another incident when he was in Orchha, a small but beautiful location in Madhya Pradesh, where he stayed in the Madhya Pradesh Tourism Hotel. When he enquired about Ashwani Lohani without revealing that he was a friend, to his pleasure the staff present there started talking at length about Ashwani Lohani. He says, "There was so much reverence attached to his name that I felt a surge of pride and admiration for my schoolmate. People really looked up to him and that's the marker of a great person, who commands respect even in his absence!"

He tells about another occasion during the alumni meet they organised. He said, "Ashwani came all the way to be a part of the meet. He was so modest and unpretentious. We were all so proud of him that he was from our school and somebody from our batch had reached such a position and was doing wonderfully well in changing each and every department he worked in. The teachers were delighted and overjoyed to see him and meet their student who they couldn't stop gushing about. Most endearing was to see his humility despite reaching such high positions and amongst us, he was just like the olden days," he mentioned, filled with nostalgia.

What else a person wants in life – respect from friends and teachers.

* * *

Ashwani Lohani is still working. That surprised me as most of the people of his age want to relax and enjoy retired life, away from the hassles of everyday challenges. But he is different.

"Passion is the fuel for continuous efforts. Never lose the passion to work. That comes from physical, mental and spiritual fitness."

I asked him, “Don’t you get tired working so much?”

“I feel 40, have the physical fitness of 20 and am actually 60. Maybe I still have many years of slogging left in me, yet the intense desire to contribute to this wonderful nation of ours, and God willing and health permitting, this desire would keep me working regardless.”

“What do you feel about being head of so many organisations? You have so much to tell us.”

“It was almost the same everywhere, be it India Tourism Development Corporation, Madhya Pradesh State Tourism Development Corporation, Air India and now railways – what a journey it has been that despite my constrained capabilities, I was placed as the head honcho of these great organisations. On 31 December 2018, I walked out of the hallowed portals of the Rail Bhawan – a satisfied soul ready to relax in the sun and bask in the reflected glory that head honcho’s get regardless of their contribution. And the only thought at that moment was gratitude for the mercy of the Almighty who gave me many opportunities to serve this great nation.”

“So, finally how do you conclude your work so far?”

“It has been a great learning, almost 39 years of it, with the diversity of the federal government, state government, a hotel company, a tourism company, an aviation company and the largest organisation of the world, all providing different yet exciting arenas. All were different yet the same. The outputs were different, yet the inputs were almost the same and why not, it is almost always about handling the three M’s within a defined time-frame, all synchronised to achieve the desired objective."

* * *

Leadership is about being effective and enlightened. He is one of the most ethical persons I have known. He gets things done. He's a doer! He is the most humble person, especially about his achievements. How a person conducts himself with his juniors speaks a lot about him. Whenever any issue with the highest or lowest person came up, he gave a patient hearing to everybody, irrespective of his status. When he was CMD, Tourism, his audacious goals were splashed across the white board in his room for everybody to see. They were his goals and he reminded himself every day through this visual medium. He is one of the finest people that exists, extremely hard working and accomplished.

With four engineering degrees, he was one of the most knowledgeable leaders anybody could hope for. While he was the Divisional Regional Manager in railways, he made sure that punctuality and cleanliness of the trains was topmost on his agenda. His passion for work is unmatchable and his energy infectious. During his term in MP Tourism, once he was at Hotel Ashok where he clearly remembers saying, "*Mai yahan free ka khana nahi khaunga*."

This was his way of announcing how driven he was for results and not benefits. The result of all his endeavours are there for everybody to see. He got two tenures in Air India which is evidence of the work put in by him due to which he got the extension. The results

"Integrity and honesty are not just words but ideals to emulate and act on."

were for everybody to see; he was able to make positive changes. He walked the talk - that was his motto! This is something which is lacking today. He does what he says he will; he's a team player, very convincing and persuasive.

□

Conclusion

With so many organisations and people we can get to the fact that there are some basic qualities which are instrumental in making a common person become special. That's what I learned from the interactions I had with Ashwani Lohani. I always wondered what made him so special! Why do people give him such high regard? Why do people hold him in such great esteem? What made him turn around every organisation he worked for?

I got answers to all of these questions and I am sure this will help you in developing a greater understanding of the style of management that makes a person not only successful, but successful with humility and regard for every human life and make every person feel important and a sense of belongingness that inspires action. This is his secret style of management. This is the magic he carried from one place to another. This led him to turn around the organisations and make them shine.

We can conclude with this example that to be a leader one needs to work holistically. Rome was not built in a day, so is true about the character of a successful man

"One needs to move from being hopeless to being proactive. Tough time never lasts but tough people do."

and his personality. It is a result of several efforts in the right direction. We all know this. The only thing required for us to be like him is to put sustained effort in the right direction.

This requires one to work in an incremental manner. We need to have faith that whatever we are doing would bring us close to the target we have set for ourselves. As one keeps on working with the goal in sight, one can definitely reach there. One of the best examples before us is India's soft landing on the moon with the success of Chandrayaan-3. It required many years of sustained organisational efforts without losing sight of the target – three missions and sacrifices done by many scientists to finally reach the moon. Lohani's example too tells us that the success he achieved and the respect he won with his work is a result of sustained effort, despite setbacks. He couldn't have become the one he is today in a day alone.

□□□